CONFRONTATION!

"Creech, you have trespassed the hell out of my property and taken branded stock," said Jonathan.

Creech, yellow-eyed and cautious, hesitated. "One or two brands taken by mistake don't make a man a rustler."

"Boy, till now I only passed the word, but it's had time to get around. You must be pretty strange around here. Chuck your guns and light down."

"Not me. I ain't giving up my gun nowise."

"Slack off, Kamas," Creech said. "You'll suit yourself, mister, but this ain't smart."

The blond youth's face tightened. "I ain't a-going on foot, Jim."

He pawed at his gun, and Jonathan brought his Navy Colt level and pulled the trigger. The cap misfired, and Kamas's weapon was swinging up to bear. Suddenly the bellow of another shot rang out. . . .

BITTER GRASS

Theodore V. Olsen

PUBLISHED BY POCKET BOOKS NEW YORK

POCKET BOOKS, a Simon & Schuster division of
GULF & WESTERN CORPORATION
1230 Avenue of the Americas, New York, N Y 10020

ISBN: 0-671-83539-4

First Pocket Books printing September, 1980

10 9 8 7 6 5 4 3 2 1

POCKET and colophon are trademarks of Simon & Schuster.

Printed in the U.S.A.

BITTER GRASS

1

ALEX MCKENNA PAUSED IN HIS RESTLESS CIR-
cling of the small, grubby orderly room, halting by a
window. He looked out on a bare stretch of dirt
compound and, beyond that, the palisaded wall of a
military stockade. Hot sunlight slatted through the
flyblown glass against his face as, hands clasped at his
back, he held his eyes on the stockade's south gate,
curbing a vast impatience. *Four years,* he thought, *and
two of them in this place.* A man was bound to be
changed, even a man like Jonathan Trask.

The prison superintendent's orderly, sprawled in his
chair, watched him with a brash, amused impudence.
"Pick up that leg in the war, Red?"

Alex glanced at the speaker. He was a callow young
weed wearing a corporal's chevrons on his neat tunic,
and Alex easily hid his annoyance which stemmed not
from the reference to leg, after all, but to his hair.
There were things a man learned to live with, and a
gimpy right leg was one. Stiff only from the knee down,
its limp was not too noticeable unless he was tired and
used up, as he was now.

In most other ways Alex McKenna made hardly an
impressive figure. At twenty-two, he stood perhaps six
inches above five feet, and he was slight. One might
think frail, but his light body was trim with wiry muscle;
except for his limp his movements held a spare, relaxed

grace. His dark suit was shabby and ill-cut, seedy and
stained from days of stage travel, with a rumpled,
slept-in look. The only memorable detail of his appearance besides the limp was his hair, thick and bright red,
which burred out from beneath his hat in shaggy
fantails. His face was thin and angular, its freckles
almost lost in a deep weatherburn, and was slurred by a
week's growth of fiery whiskers. His eyes were a deep
shade of blue that easily took on an engaging if wry
twinkle, and his strong Scot's jaw thrust out to a slight
forward cant of his head and held a latent stubbornness.

Without reply now, he eyed the immaculate corporal
long enough to make his brash grin turn stiff and waxy.
Then gave a pleasant answer: "No, not in the war."

"You borned with it?"

"No."

Swinging back to the window, he left the corporal
with his mouth foolishly open. A couple of sentries
were dragging open the south gate of the stockade, and
now three men came out. One was a blue-clad trooper,
his rifle shouldered, stepping behind a gaunt, bearded
man in ragged home-spuns who towered inches above
him. Ahead of them marched the paunchy prison
super, Captain Bissell.

Jonathan, Alex thought. *My Lord.*

The corporal had come to stand by Alex' shoulder,
peering out too. He clucked his tongue mildly.
"Boiled-looking, ain't he? Been in The Box, you can
tell. That's a dingus the Cap'n thought up his own self.
It is like a coffin, sort of, only made of steel with the lid
punched full of holes so's the air can get in. Sun too.
'Long about midday a body locked inside starts roasting
to a turn. After a day in that, a man ain't got the juices
left for kicking up a ruckus, I tell you."

"Shut up." Alex spoke without thinking; he realized

that his jaw was knotted with strain. The corporal chuckled agreeably and went back to his desk.

Jonathan was walking like a man in a trance, placing his stiff-legged steps with care; the fingers of his hands were splayed by his thighs as if he were slightly groping at each stride. The captain walked heavily slow, yet twice Jonathan stumbled and nearly fell. But his back was ramrod-straight and his head was high, and Alex thought, *No saying yet whether there is change, but you know for sure what is still there.*

Captain Bissell came through the door now, then Jonathan, and Alex turned from the window to see his face. Jonathan stood tall in the small room; somehow he filled it and washed out any other presence. His ink-black hair was long and matted; his clothes were grimy rags that showed patches of sunburned dirty skin, and the prison reek of unwashed bodies and offal and sickness made a quiet poison in the close room. His face had a red, broiled look; so did his large, big-knuckled hands, and he kept flexing the fingers. His pale gray eyes were slitted and blinking between swollen lids, for coming into the sudden gloom had almost blinded him.

"Jonathan." Alex' tongue felt thick and strange around the name, and he did not expect the quick recognition that came. He was standing in shadow well to Jonathan's right so that the big man had not noticed him on entering.

"Alex. My God, that really you, boy? Why, you red-headed ol' squirt! Alex—!"

Jonathan's black scrub of beard split to his grin as he started for Alex McKenna, but the guard brought him to a rough halt with a rifle barrel across the belly.

Captain Bissell said with a savage officiousness, "You can talk with him here." The captain was a red-faced turkey cock of a man, short and rotund, who kept hitching up his sagging belt for comfort. The heavy saber he wore as a wistful badge of dignity persisted in banging against nearly everything. "The guard will remain with you. Perkins, come in here," the captain said, and wheeled heavily into his office, his saber clanking on the doorjamb, followed by the orderly.

The guard put his back against the wall, his rifle up, and Jonathan grinned at Alex and raised his sun-raw hands. "Don't mind if I don't shake hands. Mine ain't in much shape."

The room was innocent of furniture except for the orderly's battered table-desk and two chairs. They sat, Jonathan saying quietly, "Hey, boy. God, it's good to see your ugly face. How is everyone? You heard?"

"Haven't you?"

"Not in a good four months." Jonathan scowled at his hands delicately palm-flat on the scarred table. "Any way that bastard super can make life hell for reb prisoners, he does, and maybe the best way he come up with was cutting off all word from their families a spell back." His somber eyes coalesced with little kindling lights as he leaned forward. "Mercy. How is she, boy? You ever hear that?"

"Mercy?"

"Mercy Killgrew." Impatience came like a shadow and darkened his gaze. "What about her? Is something happened?"

Alex said slowly, "She's well, last I heard," and thinking, *Mercy Killgrew. Then he doesn't know. But that was way before his mail was cut off . . . so they never told him. Should I, now?*

Thoughtfully he studied Jonathan's face, as if seeking his answer there. He remembered the last time he had seen this face, on that June morning when the Matheson County Company of Volunteers had set out from Katytown, the county seat, for San Antonio and service in the Army of the Confederacy. A brave sight in their rough homespuns and cowhide boots, yet wearing a rakish air with their colorful cow-hunt hats and flanked by their nattily uniformed officers and flagbearers. And Alex remembered standing in the crowd of cheering Texans with the Trask family and watching Jonathan's broad laughing face, smooth with youth and full of the great bursting exuberance of his nature, waving them goodbye with a sweep of his old hat which, though he was only nineteen, had borne the colors of ten years' service in the cow hunts. Beside him the thin, serious face of his brother Paul who at eighteen had been the only one of the three remaining Trask boys old enough for service. And the undisguised longing in the face of fierce, righteous Gideon Trask, the father, chafing to join them and restrained not by his fifty-eight years but by fortune's hostages of an ailing wife and two young sons.

But four more years and what seemed like another life lay between that morning and today. And that Jonathan had been a smooth-faced boy; this was a man, seasoned by maturity and war. His brow was high and strong above eyes like jagged black pebbles. His nose curved in a craggy beak to a fierce black bristle beard blurring a bellicose jut of jaw that swept into a short, powerful neck and gaunt, sloping shoulders ridged with heavy muscle. Only his mouth was clearly defined, the long lower lip holding a surprisingly sensitive pout. Paul had the identical tremulous droop to his mouth, but it exactly fitted Paul's morbid sensitized nature. In Jonathan this hint as of some obscure raw nerve in his personality had always seemed incongruous. Behind all this, his vital and volatile nature seemed to bubble as ever, undimmed by war or prison. He looked older and harder, and no other change was discernible.

Alex roused himself sharply, thinking, *Get on with it,*

and took from his pocket the two documents he had carried across half the country, laying them on the table.

"What's those?"

"One is a special order for your release. The other is a standard military parole slip." Again Jonathan's face darkened, but Alex raised his hand. "Hold up. I know about all that. But your ma could be dying. Mercy said so in a letter to me. I went to a sight of trouble getting this order so I could fetch you along on my way home."

Jonathan's glance burned steadily on him. "Could be another false alarm."

"It could be," Alex conceded. 'Liza Trask had been sickly and periodically invalided for many years; the family had long been resigned to the knowledge that any one of her recurring "attacks" might be the final one.

Knowing this, Alex could sense Jonathan's bitter hesitation, but Trask's next words veered the subject with a hard intensity. He dipped his shaggy head at the papers. "How you come by a Yankee army order?"

Alex exhaled a light sigh. "You know I headed North after you left—just before hostilities commenced?"

"I had the news. Said you was going to Boston, to this Harvard. I never did understand it."

"The law was always my big interest. You knew that, Buck."

Jonathan's grin twitched to faint life at the old nickname; then his eyes were pale frost again. "It's the notion of a Texan sitting out the whole war in the enemy camp that rankles me. We're friends, boy, which is why I'm trying to understand this."

Alex was nettled by the conversation's turn. To him, all militant patriotism had always been a childish bravado. Only his stiff limb had spared him a lifetime of maintaining the tiring façade of being indistinguishably a Southerner and a Texan and a Man. Behind all the weighty rationalizations, men hewed to their political opinions for reasons of quite mindless personal or regional sentiment. If not, the vast majorities of each side would not mechanically ally themselves to the prevailing banners. War seemed the consummate stupidity; so few were guiltless. He said slowly, "I don't see I feel much different about Texas than you, for a maybe."

"You was against the war as I recall."

"I'm against all war is why, but that doesn't change a man's feelings for his home. Look. The South has few arms-making facilities, right? A lot of the weapons your troops used were taken off dead or captured Yankees. Did you object to using Yankee facilities to fight for Texas? Then why object when I turn their means to the benefit of Texas?"

"I don't follow that, boy."

"Buck, the war's all but over. A matter of days. Lee can't break out of Richmond, and he is outnumbered better than two to one. They have won for sure, and they will be disposed to crow on one hand and bear down rough on the other. A pair of pills we'll have to swallow, bitter or not. Your way can't help Texas any more, if it ever did. She is whipped and belly-down, and setting her up proud for good and all will take knowledge and industry, not bullets and bravado. I've always believed that; it's why I went North, it's why I'm coming back with a law diploma in my possible sack."

Jonathan's gaze stayed flinty and remote. "And a Yankee military order. Don't forget that."

"I was coming to it. I had graduated from the law school at mid-term, but was staying on as an instructor of prep courses when Mercy's letter arrived. I wanted to leave right away for Texas, but thought I might obtain your release. I have a friend—we roomed together as underclassmates—whose father is high in the War Department. When I had explained the circumstances, that a man had to see his dying mother, my friend's father agreed to use his influence. In a couple of days, this order which officially renews your parole offer was in my hands."

Jonathan nodded gently. "Made yourself some Yankee friends, did you?"

Alex, keeping a rein on his prickly Scot's temper, said evenly, "That was a mistake, those Yankee friends. Otherwise I could have let you rot in this place while your mother is breathing her last."

"Sorry, boy. Sorry for that."

Jonathan rose ponderously to his feet, which brought the guard alert, watching, as he moved to the open window. The prison stockade was a little distance off, a squat and ugly scab on a land fresh with the emerald glow of spring. Beyond this, the Illinois countryside rolled under a bright young sun; the warm and silky breeze that pressed through the room smelled of growing things. Jonathan hunched his shoulders, and Alex sensed the aching, nameless need in a saddle-raised man, after two years of confinement and unbearable stenches, for the taste of open country and clean air.

Without looking around, Jonathan began to talk in a kind of grinding, savage undertone that was like cursing except for the words. Alex knew some of what he told: that through the early part of the war, Jonathan had fought with the 2nd Texas Infantry at Shiloh, Iuka, Farmington and in a dozen lesser skirmishes. It was at Shiloh by Pittsburg Landing that, hearing the wounded Paul calling his name, he had run out under fire to carry the younger Trask to safety. Paul's arm had been smashed and after surviving a butchery of amputation, he was invalided home.

Then the siege of Vicksburg, when Jonathan himself had taken a Minié ball. He was unconscious through most of the battle, and when he woke in a field hospital the color of the surgeon's uniform told him that Vicksburg had fallen. He had had no contact with his regiment after that, no news of how his comrades had fared, and not till he was on the mend had he learned that he alone of the Confederate prisoners was refusing parole. Hearing that the 2nd Texas was reorganizing its shattered ranks at Galveston, he had hoped to escape and join them, but had not succeeded then or later, after being shipped to Centralia prison in Illinois.

Alex put in mildly, "As I have it, all the rebel prisoners taken at Vicksburg in '63 were offered parole." He tapped his finger on the oblong paper beside the military order. "Didn't they ask you to sign a parole slip like this one?"

"Maybe my mark." Jonathan barely glanced at the slip. "You know I can't write. Read either. Does it say like the one a Yankee officer read off at Vicksburg? About them terms of . . . of capitulation?"

Alex raised his brows and picked up the paper, reading aloud: "'. . . give this my solemn parole under oath—that I will not take up arms against the United States, nor serve in any military or constabulary force in any fort, garrison or field work held by the Confederate States of America against the United States of America, nor as guard of prisoners, depots or stores, nor discharge any duties usually performed by officers or soldiers against the United States of America until duly exchanged by the proper authorities.'"

"God damn it, boy." Abruptly Jonathan swung from the window, sweeping his fingers through his matted hair. "That don't leave a man fixed but to swat flies and wish Yankees dead. Fancy ain't fighting, and I didn't hone on signing that away. Meant to bide my time and bust out of this Christ-bitten hole. I gave myself a vow I wouldn't take no Yankee parole while Texas was fighting Yankees. Well, they're fighting on now, beat or not."

Almost Alex could smile at that. For if he did not understand why a man would accept the soul-destroying hell of a military prison to make his point with himself alone, he understood Jonathan Trask only too well. Even when they were boys, it had been just so: once Jonathan set himself to any goal, big or little, he would pursue it at all costs, with a savage and insensate determination.

After a moment, though, Alex said only, "Forget your damned pride for once. You've made your point, and the fighting's nearly ended. A week or two more, what does that matter?" More gently he added, "Buck, you would not forgive yourself if she dies now and you could have been there."

"Could be it'll turn out another false alarm," Jonathan muttered again, then: "No easier on you, eh, boy? She's 'most as much ma as you ever known, too."

Alex only nodded. Whenever he thought of what he owed Gideon and 'Liza and the other Trasks, words became inadequate and puerile. There was an irony in this, since over the past four years he had set out to expunge the backcountry from his speech, to master the spoken and written word. Yet all the intensity he had applied to his law studies had been toward the end of bending his wit and learning to the service of the people who had made him one of their own.

Jonathan said glumly now, "You knew how this had to go, boy," said stridently lifted his voice: *"Yankee!"*

Captain Bissell exited from his office almost at once, then hauled up with a cold and breathless glare.

Jonathan drawled, "Bet the old stockade won't seem the same without me around, Cap'n."

With a wild and harried dignity, Captain Bissell strode to the table, his saber banging on its leg, and glanced at the documents which he had already perused thoroughly. He said as if the words had a bad taste, "All he has to do is sign this parole slip in my presence. I'd say you know some important people, Mr. McKenna."

"Let's say a friend has an important friend," Alex said coldly. "I'm not too conversant with military law, Captain, or I would quote the letter of whatever covers brutality to prisoners of war."

"Brutality—?" Bissell's jowlish jaw sagged and then snapped like a trap. "Damn it, sir! This unregenerate ruffian went out of his way to make a damned nuisance of himself—sabotaging discipline, instigating riots, organizing prison breaks. Why, he tried an even dozen times to break out and succeeded twice, only to be run down by guards and dogs. He forced me repeatedly to inflict the most drastic punishments—and when I did, he *laughed* at me—"

Captain Bissell was floundering in his raging catalogue of Jonathan's sins; and now Jonathan chuckled, a sound full-throated and rolling and hearty. He stood high and spraddle-legged and somehow indomitable in his rags and filth. The captain blanched faintly; his jowls shook. He had done his worst, in a place already befouled by privation and disease and near-starvation, to break this man who would not break.

"Aw shoot, Cap'n. . . ." Jonathan sounded at once good-natured and gently sly. "You-all got to make it down to Texas one time, y'hear? Damned if I don't hone to show you some grand ol' Secesh hospitality."

Older and harder and essentially unchanged: this was Jonathan Trask, laughing away a two-years' experience that should have destroyed him inside and out, spirit and body. But then the real acid test for him still lay ahead, Alex knew, as surely as he knew the depth of Jonathan's love for Mercy Killgrew. Knowing too what Jonathan did not: that for well over a year, Mercy had been married to Paul Trask, the brother whose life Jonathan had saved at Shiloh.

2

ALEX' SMALL HOARD OF YANKEE GOLD AND greenbacks outfitted them with a couple of tough and rangy nags that were short on looks but to a horseman's trained eye long-stayers, and two scarred and serviceable saddles. A quantity of dried foods, a few utensils, and two good secondhand Sharps rifles and two Navy Colts completed their equipment. In addition Alex changed his suit, and Jonathan his prison rags, for a cotton shirt, sturdy kersey trousers, a slouch hat, and a pair of stout boots for each.

The two of them made good time as they followed the thaw-rutted roads into Missouri. Here the Yankee patrols were out in force, cleaning up pockets of resistance, the guerrilla bands of Redlegs and Jayhawkers. More than once Jonathan and Alex were halted on the road and forced to produce identification. Jonathan's parole slip was always enough to pass him. From one such patrol they got the only several-days-old news of the surrender of Appomattox. And it was really over. . . .

Ahead lay a homecoming that a man might well wish to put off, a dying woman who was mother to one, foster-mother to the other. Ahead too lay a defeated and impoverished land. But that land was Texas, and for all their somber thoughts a high anticipation gripped them. They talked to while away the hours; they renewed an old strange bond of friendship that was not forgotten, but blurred around the edges.

And finally home was near: the familiar shaggy sedgegrass prairies of the Yegua country; the groves of pecan trees and liveoak; the ancient buffalo wallows filled by the spring rains where the thousands of wild ducks and curlews and whooping cranes from the Dakotas and Canada wintered. Here were the lonely creek bottoms where as boys they had hunted red squirrels and quail, deer and wild turkey, and the maned giant "lofer" wolves; where they had wetted lines in pooling backwaters full of catfish and bream and perch; where occasional alligators still basked in the sun; where wild longhorns ran the brush as always, but seemingly wilder than ever.

Beyond the West Yegua Creek crossing, as they neared the Brushy Creek and home, Alex was wondering, *Should I tell him about Mercy and Paul now?* It might be kinder to prepare him. Alex briefly chased that ragged impulse and let it die unheeded as Jonathan pointed at a prairie island, a liveoak motte isolated to the west. "Remember that, boy? Pa found you hard by there."

Actually he had been barely old enough to remember, but it was a day that Alex McKenna would never forget. . . .

His father, Rob McKenna, had been a Scotch-Irish immigrant whose wanderings had brought him into the piney woods of northern Louisiana, where he had married and quickly produced a sizable family. His thirst for wild and wide-open places was whetted by a talk with a footloose plainsman fresh out of Texas, and in the spring of 1849 the McKennas had pulled up stakes and, looking for a place to settle, had followed the San Antonio Road to the River Colorado and swung north toward the Yegua Creek country.

They had made night camp at the edge of a grove not far from the creek when six-year-old Alex, off playing in the trees, had heard a commotion. He remembered running toward the camp and falling, his head striking a root, and then for a long time, nothing at all. Coming to, he had found the charred, smoking wreckage of the wagon, the slaughtered oxen, the butchered bodies of his family, father and mother, three sisters and a baby brother. Then a time of blank and muddy shock.

Gideon' Trask and his *vaqueros*, attracted by the smoke, found him the next day. After a simple burial and service, Gideon had brought the shock-silent boy home to his ranch on the Brushy. Later it was learned that a half-dozen drunken Comanches had committed the massacre.

The slow, healing weeks as his mind gradually returned from some dark and withdrawn place were an uncertain blur in his memory. Yet here and there he could find patches of vivid rememberance. There were only two Trask sons then, Jonathan being the older by a year and Paul of an age with Alex. He and the younger Trask brother had been friendly almost from the first; it was Paul whose shy, moody ways had struck some kindred spark, and Paul's friendship, as much as the kindness of 'Liza Trask, then heavy with her third child, her warm heart overflowing with more affection than she could lavish on a husband and two sons, had drawn the orphaned Alex into the Trask circle. Gideon, by native manner brusque and austere, was harder to know, but he had treated Alex exactly like one of his sons.

Jonathan was the unreachable one, though he alone of the Trasks had been boisterous and outgoing. The antagonism between him and Alex had never approached hatred or even strong dislike, yet there had been from the first a perplexing, almost instinctive friction. It was like the stiff-backed sidling and sniffing out of two stranger dogs trying to get each other's measure and finding only the chasm that lies between two inherently opposed personalities.

Jonathan had been big and heavy for his years; often and superciliously and quite deliberately, whenever there was no danger of being caught out, he would lay for the slight, bony Alex and provoke him to fights by giving orders which Alex would never obey. He was sly enough never to leave a bruise where it would show, and Alex would never tattle. Always he had fought back with an insensate stubbornness, silent and tearless and tight-lipped, till he was too licked to continue. (Oddly, in this way alone they were alike, and the fact of meeting his stubborn match may have been a red goad to Jonathan, Alex often thought.)

Still, in spite of personalities and a bad beginning, they had become friends. All because of one event in a single day, another day that would always stick fast with Alex McKenna.

The Yegua cow and mustang hunters always rendezvoused at Jim Killgrew's place, located centrally between the Brushy and Yegua creeks. Here they had sunk hardwood posts, lashing them together with rawhide to form big holding corrals. The native longhorns were hell to catch, and hunting them for beef and hides presented little less difficulty. In open country it was almost impossible to get within musket range of these wild cattle, while they were airily at home in the brush. But they provided the main source of meat and, just as important, tallow, and the tough hides which furnished the settlers with everything from *chaparejo* pants to chairseat lacings.

The Trask boys and Alex were participating in the cow hunts before they turned ten, and after a couple years' apprenticeship each was expected to carry a grown man's workload. Paul had nurtured a sullen discontent, for he never did take suitably to range work. Alex, though, had liked the color and excitement of the hunts, and had made up in determination and drive what he lacked in size and strength.

But it was Jonathan who seemed most in his proper element, as much as a duck on water. By the age of eight he had the job of leading the "bell mare," a tote horse that carried all the gear of the cowhunters. By eleven he was popping the wildest *cimaronnes* out of the worst brush, catching and tying like a seasoned hand. He could toss a tight swift loop over a brushrunner's muzzle and one horn, or over a heel, with equal facility. He also used his increased status to bully Alex, who now led the bell mare. In addition to toting gear, the animal provided a gathering point at meals and night camp for the scattered hunters, a row of tin cups strong on its rope being rattled in summons. Jonathan would mercilessly keep him ringing the primitive "bell" until Alex thought his aching arm would fall off.

About this time Jonathan had learned a game called *colear* from the Mexican *vaqueros* who outnumbered the Anglos on the hunt crews. *Colear* was running your horse alongside a bolting longhorn, getting a hold on the animal's tail and taking a swift single dally around the flat saddle horn, then heading off at right angles so that the cow was flipped off its feet in full stride. It was a practice sternly discouraged by Gideon, as too many cattle were lost to broken legs and snapped vertabrae. However Jonathan, undaunted, would often tackle the reckless game when he was alone or only Paul or Alex were around to see.

This was the case on one day during the spring of

1854, when Alex was eleven and Jonathan just turned twelve. The year's first hunt was almost over, and the bulk of the district cowhunters were engaged in hazing their catches to the Killgrew corrals for the branding, earmarking and, in the case of bulls, castration.

Jonathan, however, had ridden off some distance from the headquarters that day to take a last whirl at hunting down El Rojo, an ancient steer for whom he nursed a particular grudge. El Rojo was a giant bull with needle-pointed horns and slatty flanks furrowed by the crisscrossed scars of a hundred vicissitudes. For years he had successfully eluded the guns and nooses of the hunters; he was utterly unregenerate, totally vicious, and wily as old Nick. He knew the bottoms and draws better than any settler, where the most impenetrable cover was and when to seek it. Jonathan had tried off and on for a year to run him down, with a spectacular lack of success.

Today, determined not to quit until he had secured the wild one, Jonathan was skirting the creek-bottom thickets, keeping his eyes open. To Alex, he had delegated the task of following with the yoke of oxen that would drag the red steer to the holding corrals when he was taken. Now and then Jonathan would take out his mounting impatience on his companion, railing at him abusively. "God damn you, boy," he would shout, "don't hang back on me. Get along behind me and stay close."

Alex was quite close behind him when El Rojo made a sudden dash from a thicket where he had been standing immobile until the two riders were uncomfortably near. He crashed away into deeper brush, but Jonathan knew the terrain too, and he heeled his bay into a run, cutting El Rojo off and swerving him back to the open.

Heart pounding, Alex stood high in his stirrups and watched as Jonathan expertly tailed up the giant running brute, whirling out the plaited coils of his *riata*. And then, as Alex had fully expected would be the case, Jonathan was unable to resist the challenge posed by tailing El Rojo clear of brush on a straightaway run. Discarding his rawhide lariat, he lay flat to his bay's withers and urged him alongside the steer.

In an instant the stringy tail was in Jonathan's grasp and almost in the same moment he had dallied and was spurring offside to achieve the swift, deadly *colear* that would snap El Rojo clear off his feet.

But El Rojo, by chance or design or instinct, broke his straight run at the same time, pivoting in a direction that was sufficiently opposite to Jonathan's turn to offset his move. In the next confused instant, Alex saw horse and boy and steer down in the moiling dust. The squealing bay was struggling with a broken foreleg; Jonathan was crawling to his hands and knees, dazed.

The red steer lunged to his feet snorting; he wheeled off a short ways and turning, charged down on the half-stunned youth. Alex had not even hesitated as El Rojo had scrambled up; already onto the steer's next move, he put his own mount into a hurtling run that would thrust him across El Rojo's path, between the steer and Jonathan.

Proudly worn in the bright sash around Alex' narrow middle was the shiny cap-and-ball Colt that had been a gift from his foster parents last birthday. Now he yanked it free and pumped two shots at El Rojo as he neared him. They did not slow the big steer by a jot, and in the next moment Alex saw that his angle and momentum were carrying his mount and El Rojo into imminent collision. A twitch of the rein could have turned him safely aside, but Alex bore stubbornly

side-on to the steer. He sent a shot behind the bunched
muscles of El Rojo's forehock.

Then the surging and savage impact; he felt himself
lifted clear of saddle. The earth pinwheeled and
smashed him across the back, driving the breath from
him. Next the red and shocking agony of his leg being
inexplicably crushed and his own scream mercifully
throttled by sudden blackness. . . .

The last bullet that Alex had fired found El Rojo's
heart and the great brute had gone into a dying fall
even as Alex's plucky little cowpony lunged into him.
The boy had been thrown clear, but his pony had
immediately cartwheeled onward over the downed
steer. The rawhide-rigged saddle, backed by the pony's
plunging weight, had come down across Alex's outstretched leg. The lower limb was crushed between the
solid cantle and the hard earth.

Jonathan, to do him justice, could not have done
more toward making amends during the pain-wracked
weeks that followed. At first only his keen sense of debt
had bridged them; from this bond had grown, finally,
friendship. Yet to this day, Alex could not think back
on that natural friction between their stubbornly differ-
ing personalities without realizing that the passing years
would have evolved it into enmity, except for the gap
being artificially crossed by that sudden and dramatic
accident. . . .

Jonathan's soft whoop yanked him from the mood.
They had topped a shallow ridge which stretched for a
good mile or more parallel to the Brushy's winding
course, but set well back on the black bottomlands
above its low, willowchoked bank.

When Gideon had first come on this creek bottom
twenty years ago, the site of his future home had taken

his eye at once. As an Austin colonist, he had been allotted a headright league of land that comprised a vast wedge between the Yegua and Brushy creeks. Here, about midway between ridge and creek bank flourished a small park of post oaks and walnuts, and here he had cleared land for his buildings. After completing the house- and shed-raising, with the neighbors' help, he had broken up the virgin bottom-land with his turning plow for plantings of corn and potatoes and a little cotton. Except for improvements, the homesite had changed little over the years; the grove and the rambling cabin, whose original structure now boasted two flanking wings, were the same.

But Alex' first bursting lift of spirit choked back in his chest. The fields were barren and untilled, overrun with a rank tangle of weeds and brush; the buildings had a stark and silent appearance like desertion, as if they had grown old waiting for the return of tenants who had gone away long ago.

"There she is, boy," Jonathan shouted huskily, "there she is all over, by God," his voice hushing away then as his face sobered to the thought of why they had returned. He set the spurs lightly and put his rangy nag down the slope at a swift, reaching gait.

As they neared the buildings, Alex noticed how the whole place had gained a prideless, rundown look. The corrals were fouled, fences were broken and gaping, and stray pieces of gear made a careless litter of the yard. The dark and weathered buildings were intact, built for a lifetime, but the split-shake roofs were in sad disrepair, and the cabin's stone chimney was crumbling at the base. Plain neglect had crept like a shabby fungus over the place.

Dismounting, they crossed the sagging porch and entered the house. The parlor, with its big stone fireplace and dark heavy furniture, was still neatly kept. "Pa!" Jonathan called softly. "Mercy? Cort, Liam, where are you-all? Ma?"

A man came to a doorway, shuffling and halting there. Once a big man, he was now stooped and gaunt. Alex felt a bitter shock, for Gideon Trask had aged incredibly in these few years. His granite face had eroded into a wasted, deeply incised slackness, and his thick mane of gray-shot black hair was almost white. His eyes, once hard and bright, seemed to retreat; and now Alex had the startled realization that Jonathan had matured to strikingly resemble the man his father had been.

Gideon's eyes faintly questioned, holding no recognition. "Gentlemen?" he said softly.

"Pa." Jonathan went to him and took him by the shoulders. "It's me—us—me and Alex. I'm Jonathan, Pa."

"Jonathan . . . no. Jonathan was my boy. Dead boy . . . Vicksburg."

Jonathan said, "My Lord," and let his hands drop. His eyes moved past his father to the doorway where Samantha had appeared, quiet as a shadow. She was a tall, fierce-natured Haitian whose spirit had never been cowed by whip or chain. Her thin, aquiline features still hinted at the wild beauty that, as an Afro-Indian and a slave, had cursed her youth.

She did not greet them; her face was carved mahogany as she said tonelessly, "He's been that way since old Mis'ress died, but ain't nothing wrong in his head." Watching their faces, Samantha paused; her impassive features did not faintly change. "See you didn't know. It was a good three weeks ago." She nodded toward a window. "We laid Mis'ress 'Liza over yonder under that biggest walnut. The Rev'rend Mister Boggs said some powerful words." Her eyes glittered faintly; she gently nodded her head. "They carried one strong *juju* on them, them words."

Jonathan half-wheeled toward the doorway, but then halted, his head bowed. Finally he looked slowly at his father, then at Samantha with a questioning scowl. "What's that about nothing wrong in his head?"

Wordlessly she pointed at a half-empty bottle of whiskey on the fireplace mantel, as Gideon walked unsteadily to an armchair and fell slackly into it. His head rolled sidelong on his shoulder; he snored. Alex could not believe it; there was nothing about this malleable shambles of a man to remind him of big, vital Gideon Trask, the man to whom he owed more than his life.

"He got started like that when he knowed your ma was dying," Samantha said matter-of-factly. "Now you and Mister Alex are back, maybe he be better."

"Where is Mercy? My brothers?"

"Mister Paul and the boys is out hunting for meat. Wild beef is all this table is seen for a hard spell. Miss Mercy, she out walking somewheres."

Without another word, Jonathan wheeled and tramped out of the house. Alex came to the doorway and watched him swing big-shouldered across the yard, calling Mercy Killgrew's name. A flash of color near the creek bank, and a woman's slender form stepped from the fringing willows. She came to a halt as Jonathan called again. Her face, now turning his way, went as colorless as the white blossoms heaped in her upheld apron. She let go the apron and all the fresh-cut water blooms fell unnoticed to the ground. Her lips trembled, forming his name. Jonathan, with a glad soft, "Mercy," reached her in a dozen long steps.

Even as his face dipped, his hands on her arms, she began struggling, twisting her face away. "No, Jonathan—no, listen to me, please—" It was a check on his rough eagerness. And Alex, unwilling to be witness to the destruction of a man's dream, turned back into the house.

3

SAMANTHA HAD BEEN STANDING SOMEWHAT BE-
hind him, looking on. Her eyes gleamed darkly in her
strong, handsome face. "Plenty evil gwine come 'count
of this business." She touched the protective *gris-gris*
hung on a rawhide thong about her neck. "Best you
don't smile, now, 'bout what you don't understand,
mister."

"As a respecter of all faiths," Alex said dryly, "I am
duly appreciative of voodos. Especially the optimism."
He eyed her thoughtfully. Years ago Gideon Trask had
bought Samantha from a brutal wharf overseer in New
Orleans, such an act of charitable pity as a Christian
man might bestow on any dumb, suffering animal. But
neither blows nor charity could make an obsequious,
head-bobbing Auntie of Samantha. Because she was an
extremely good worker, the Trasks had grudgingly
tolerated her uppity ways, as they would those of an
ingrate pup or a fool savage unable to learn better.

Alex said mildly, "Santhy, it's long past the time for
breaking ground. Why aren't those fields sowed?"

The fine flare of her nostrils deepened. "Old Mas'r,
you think he work now? Mister Paul can't plow any
more, and that Cort boy, you can lay he won't if he can
be running the brush somewheres."

From outside came the lift of Jonathan's strident and

31

angry voice, "All right—all right," and Alex saw him
tramp blindly away down the creek bank. Mercy stood
looking after him, then stooped and slowly gathered up
the blossoms she had dropped. She went on across the
clearing and halted by the gravemound beneath the
spreading shade of the biggest walnut. Kneeling, she
laid the flowers by the crude headboard, arranging
them.

Alex left the house and crossed to the walnut grove.
For a moment he stood by 'Liza Trask's grave with
bowed head, absorbed in a tribute of good memories to
the woman who, had been his mother in all but fact.
And then he had to meet Mercy's gaze; her eyes were
large with reproach.

"Hello, Mercy."

"Alex . . . you could have told him, in all those days
you was together. I know, we should have got him word
sometime, but him bursting in all a-sudden like this
. . . you could have spared me that."

Alex shook his head. "About that, I'm sorry. But
none of it was my place to say. You and Paul. . . ."

"Are the culprits. Oh Lord God, what a terrible,
terrible mistake." She came to her feet and pressed her
cheek to the huge walnut, and struck her palm once
against the bark, an anguished, helpless gesture. "Oh
Alex, the look in his eyes . . . like watching a little boy
getting hurt to the quick and trying . . . trying so hard
to understand what he can't."

Mutely Alex watched her, hoping she would not cry.
She straightened after a moment, her shoulders back,
and he felt relieved and a little ashamed of it.

The Killgrews had been the Trasks' closest neighbors, and Alex remembered how even as children, the
attraction between Jonathan and Mercy had been a
spontaneous and inevitable quality. As they had grown
up, Paul had offered a spirited rivalry for a time, but

even then it had been all Mercy for Jonathan, Jonathan
for Mercy, a fact nobody else ever questioned. After
typhus had taken both Jim Killgrew and his wife six
years ago, she had come to live with the Trasks, making
her in a very real way Alex' orphan-sister. She looked
almost as he remembered, small and pert and wearing a
faced crinoline with the grace of a young princess. The
smooth black wings of her brushed-back hair flanked an
oval, piquant face which was still unwontedly pale. Her
full lips were compressed with a sadness that reached
and dimmed the old flash of her eyes, and he knew that
maturity had not dulled her vivacity: rather it must
have faded from the day that the false rumor of
Jonathan's death had reached her. And he said gently
now, "I never understood exactly how you came to
think Buck was dead."

"Declare . . . I never been such a baby before." She
brushed a hand across her eyes. "Remember Lige
Manigault?"

"That fellow with an outfit just north of the Yegua?"

"Yes. He entered the 2nd Texas Volunteers with
Jonathan and Paul, and he was one of them taken at
Vicksburg who got paroled on his word not to fight
again. Well, when Lige come home, he paid me a visit
straight off. Told me he was standing square beside
Jonathan at a barricade when this shot hit—just about
tore Jonathan in half, he said." She shuddered, blinking her dark lashes. "Lige might of lied a little bit—he
was always sweet on me, and I know he hoped—but I
reckon as bad as Jonathan was hurt, he must of
honestly looked dead. I have seen it in my dreams a
hundred times, Jonathan lying all covered with blood
and a huge wound in his stomach."

"But you surely waited for word."

"Alex, I waited! . . . day after day for months. All I
could learn was that all the dead at Vicksburg were

buried in a common trench. A lot of dead soldiers couldn't be identified. And no word ever come that he'd been taken. If he had, we all figured he would of given his parole and come directly home, or maybe gone to Galveston like some others and volunteered for non-combat duty at the supply docks and warehouses. But never a word—never a word."

"He turned down parole, but he sent you word."

"Yes, a good six months after Vicksburg fell!"

"He was hurt mighty bad, Mercy, touch-and-go a long spell. That long before he was even in shape to have another fellow write for him."

"He told me . . . told me all that." She sank slowly down and sat with her back to the tree, dipping her dark head. "Paul was home, getting back on his feet after losing his arm at Shiloh, and . . . we was thrown together a good bit. Me hurting so much from Jonathan, and Paul so bitter—it was his right arm, and you know how he always hankered to be an artist."

Alex nodded soberly. One summer an itinerant photographer had stopped over at the ranch for a week. He had also been equipped with paints and canvas to capture, he had said, the color and drama of the West as no daguerreotype or ambrotype could. Paul had been fourteen, and that encounter had fixed his lodestar.

"He was always moody, and now it was worse'n ever. A body couldn't but be sorry for him. And he needed me so much—was always in love with me, even when me and Jon—" The delicate arch of her throat quivered; she drew up her knees and clasped her ankles. "For a long spell after I was sure Jonathan was dead, it didn't matter. But then I began to need too, and Paul was there. So we was married." She tilted her head, and a pure misery filled her eyes. "Alex, why? Can you tell me why?"

Alex heard a shout then, and looked over toward the corral. Three riders, just come into sight, were dropping off their horses. A boy of fifteen had whooped out, and he came over on the run, moving with a lanky adolescent grace. Halting, he grinned unabashedly, thumbs hooked in the waist of his butternut pants, then suddenly thrust out his hand. "Welcome back."

Alex smiled. "Didn't know as you'd recall me, Cort."

"Sure thing." Cortney Trask scooped back his hair, which was thick and black with the deep Trask widow's peak, from his eyes. They were pale and bold and restless, not quite insolent; there was a wiry tensile alertness about him. A second boy had sidled shyly up beside him. Cort said, "This here is Liam. Says he recalls you all right."

Alex held out his hand until Liam took it and said, "H-h-hello," stammering badly. Liam was almost two years younger than Cort, but already as tall and reaching for considerable heft. He had never been stupid; he had showed at times any child's bright curiosity. But his attention wandered like a moth; facts and names and faces drifted in and out of his mind, and his thoughts were faraway. In an aged person you would call it senility; in this child it was some nameless, everlasting daydream which to be wholly wrenched from would leave him naked and miserable. The other Trasks had always watched over him with a fierce protectiveness, and at least one of them was never far from him. Gently Alex rubbed the boy's head, then glanced at the grinning Cort and said soberly, "You notice anything unusual when you rode in?"

"Like what?" Cort demanded.

"Like two extra horses in the corral."

"Sure, yours."

"One of 'em's mine," Alex said with a grin, and

watched Cort's face alter from puzzlement to comprehension to disbelief.

"Ah, Alex. Hey, you really mean it? Is he?"

"Take a look by the creek. Last I saw—"

Whooping, Cort broke into a run, then wheeled back and caught hold of Liam and dragged him along, shouting, "Don't stand there, boy! Ol' Buck's back. Buck, hey!"

Paul Trask had come up and now he halted, watching the two boys run toward the creek. He had always stood apart from his family; Cort's blind idolizing of the absent Jonathan would not have helped matters. Now Paul stepped forward, self-consciously extending his left hand. The empty right sleeve of his cowhide jacket was rolled up and pinned at the shoulder. It was a sharp reminder of the cruelest irony of all: that probably only Jonathan's prompt action in risking his own life had saved his injured brother for the girl Jonathan loved. Briefly Alex shared the awkwardness; he had to force a smile, "Good to see you, fella."

"*You* haven't changed." Paul flicked the first word with inflection. He had his brothers' black, unruly hair, but his fair skin that burned and peeled anew each year was legacy of his brave, frail mother. He had his father's height, without Gideon's former weight and hardihood; his sad and scornful eyes that brooded at all the world betrayed a nervous and near morbid sensitivity. Alex shared with him only a wry satrical outlook, yet it had always sufficed to make Paul the Trask closest to him, and Alex had gotten on well with them all while Paul was close only to his mother.

The smile on Paul's lips nearly reached his eyes; he seemed to remember and his grip tightened. "Alex . . . good you're back." His glance shuttled briefly to Mercy. "Was that straight about you brought Buck with you?"

Alex, explaining how he had obtained Jonathan's release, sensed a fretting of cross-tension between husband and wife. Paul and Mercy watched him, not each other, and yet as he walked slowly toward the house between them, Alex had the uneasy feeling that he was talking over and around, not to them.

With his family present to look after Gideon, Samantha took her leave for the log shack beyond the fields, where she lived. Mercy prepared supper, such as it was. Beef was always available when no other meat was, so filling a man's belly was no problem. Otherwise the table she set was eloquent of the hard times on which the Trasks—and Texas—had fallen. Even an ordinary elegance of greens and good coffee was lacking: Mercy boiled up a pot of chicory and made bad biscuits from weevily flour.

They ate with the wordless concentration of hungry men and boys, except for Gideon, who had gone to sleep in his armchair; and halfway through the meal Jonathan entered at last, took his place and began to eat. His manner was dark and subdued, but not forbidding. Alex had been braced for this meeting, but when Paul said a quiet greeting and Jonathan replied in like fashion, he relaxed. The two brothers' relation had always been at best barely civil; it was at least that now.

After supper the family gathering in the parlor seemed as always. Only the old hand-carved rocker, where 'Liza Trask had spent the evenings with her basket of sewing and mending, made an empty place. Gideon had awakened, the whiskey slept off and his faculties clear. He recognized and greeted his eldest son and Alex with pleasure, but then only sat unspeaking, staring at the empty rocker with a musing, wistful indifference. Paul and Alex talked perfunctorily, telling each other of their lives since the war had separated them. Jonathan slumped in his chair, sunk in thought.

The two boys were restless because Cort was and Liam followed his example; they rolled on the floor tussling and grimacing, and finally Cort leaped to his feet.

"Hey, Mercy. Can we roast pecans?"

"You ask your pa," she said from the kitchen.

But it was Jonathan, his voice deep and quiet, who said, "Sure Cort. You roast pecans," then came from his chair in a spare movement and stalked to the fireplace. He leaned an arm on the mantel and settled his eyes on an old Doré print on the far wall, not looking at any of them. Yet his big, slouched frame commanded the room. With five words and a quietly assuming posture, he had taken the reins of Trask leadership. Gideon mused on, paying no attention. The others did, and nobody commented. Jonathan's very stance proclaimed that this was how it would be, and there was nothing else to know.

When he spoke again, his words were deliberate: "Walked for hours. Seen a goodly number of cattle within a few miles, not over a handful wearing brands."

Paul leaned forward in his chair, setting his one elbow on his knees. "There's cattle, all right, running wild over the whole country, what with most cowmen in the Army and the coast markets dead. Me and the two boys been branding what we can run down, but we got no crew and nothing to pay one. We been just hanging on, and I'm wondering if it's worth the candle."

"It is. Will be now hostilities has ceased." Jonathan inserted a twisted cigar in his teeth and bent to light an oak splinter; his gaze was smoky and speculative. "At Vicksburg I seen civilians pay seven silver dollars for a little cut of good roast. Them Eastern cities will be booming from the war. They will want good beef and will pay aplenty for it." He nodded his shaggy head at Alex, whimsically. "This lawyer we all at once know says there is no shame to using Yankee knowhow. I been pondering them words. All right. Yankee gold shines the same as anyone's." Jonathan straightened up, lighting his smoke with the ignited splinter, and he said: "We will burn the old GT brand on every God damned thing we see that moves and wears horns and a tail. When them Yankees quit crowing and start rubbing their bellies, we'll be ready. We'll start a range count tomorrow."

Paul settled back, drumming his fingers on his knee; he wore a satirical smile. "You mean me? Or Alex? You don't count or cipher 'cept on your fingers, Buck, and there is a few more than ten head out there."

Jonathan had dropped his hand, about to toss the splinter back in the fire, and now he paused and watched it smolder out, puffing gently on the cigar. *Damn Paul's mouth*, Alex thought dismally. When, as boys, Alex and Paul had given obedient if sometimes lagging attention to the studies that 'Liza had laid out for them, Jonathan in stubborn rebellion had refused the books and had taken repeated hidings for it until his despairing parents had simply given up, letting him attend exclusively to rangework as he wanted.

Now, after a moment, Jonathan only said pleasantly, "That's half right, boy. You for one." He paused deliberately. "And when you made your count, you report back to me."

The quiet challenge went over Paul's head; he merely nodded, his attention already straying to the kitchen doorway to absorb his wife's movements. He had always been indifferent to cattle and ranching and now, Alex thought, with his arm gone, all he had was Mercy; nothing else held real concern for him.

A hint of the deep slow excitement gripping Jonathan showed in the abruptness with which he stood and paced to a window. Hands clasped at his back, he stared into the night. "The name of Trask will mean something in this country—in Texas. You mark me." He said it calmly and with no doubt at all, and Alex thought of the inherent doggedness that had let him refuse parole for two nightmare years in a prison camp.

But prison had failed to scratch Jonathan's big rough ebullience. The knowledge of losing Mercy hard on the heels of his mother's death and seeing his father's manhood broken—these things had scored deeply. The blackness of his eyes seemed to tunnel back into his soul, yet gave no clue to his thoughts. Still the change was there. What was it then?

Already, with an effort of inner violence that was uniquely Jonathan Trask, he had made a wrenching acceptance of the fact that the only woman in his life was lost to him: already a new vigor and vision, a dream of empire perhaps, was possessing him. In sum, maybe that was it. In a few short hours some great and open-handed quality of Jonathan's, call it an innocence, had left him forever. Alex McKenna, loving these foster people of his as only an orphan could, knew that the old broken pattern of the family circle would be reshaped around the sudden void in Jonathan's life. Whatever filled that void would seize the direction that each life would take, good or bad.

4

In the morning, at breakfast, Jonathan told Paul to take a tally on the range south of the Brushy, while he covered Trask land north of the creek. Cort was boiling to ride with Jonathan, who crisply squelched the idea.

"Be some changes about here, boy. The place ain't fit for hogs. You and Li get to cleaning out them corrals. Ought to take you the day." He glanced at Alex. "Counselor, reckon you could spare time in the evenings to prime these tads with some book-learning?"

Cort almost wept. "You never bothered yourself with that stuff, hey Buck. Why you putting it on us?"

"It's a need is why," Jonathan said grimly. "One I'll be tending to on my own account when I got the time." He finished his chicory and stood, wiping his hands on his pants. "All right, let's all get rousting."

Paul said, "Alex, want to ride along?"

"He'll ride with me," Jonathan said. "The counselor and me got some palaver to make."

Alex was tempted to challenge the assertion, but a glance at the edge of resentment in Paul's face decided him not to say anything that might deepen the quiet rift.

The morning was bright as a blade as Jonathan and

Alex rode north from the headquarters. After a while Jonathan said, "I give a lot of study to what you said about a body needing to truckle to the times. All these woollyheads running about free as their betters now will need work, and there ain't no better workers." He paused. "That's the answer to our big problem, which is we're busted. We will take on a passel of 'em and make top hands of 'em. A few dollars and found will keep 'em happy, seeing they never got paid before."

"Not many hereabouts owned slaves."

"We'll drive a few head to N'Awleans for cash and hire us a passel of Nigras there."

As they steadily covered the dense thickets and the open grass between the mottes and bosques, Alex was astounded at the number of unbranded cows running free over the few square miles they had crossed. These longhorns were wild as deer, literally ranging in color across every spectrum of the rainbow, with great curving horns of all conceivable shapes. Most of the animals were a faded orange in color, but there were also browns and bays, duns and slates, blue and black and white and red, speckled hides and streaked hides, dark horns and light. Jonathan's method of tally had a primitive efficiency: he could count as far as ten, and on every tenth head he tied a knot in his saddle string, making every hundredth knot a double one.

The two men ranged north to the bank of the Yegua and made a wide circle back south. At midafternoon, with Alex' help, Jonathan totaled up his double knots. Even he was staggered, and then exultant. "Almost four thousand head this near to home, and not over a few wearing any one's brand. Boy, this war could turn out the best thing ever happened to us."

"*Salud* to the Trasks, then."

Jonathan eyed him askance, critically. "You're pretty much a Trask, and don't forget it. Brings me to this medicine I meant to make. All the time we was riding I never asked if you got any plans made."

Alex shrugged. "No time to settle any. When word came of your ma, I was fixing to leave for Texas within the year anyhow, but thought no more on what next. Had toyed with the idea of opening law practice in Katytown."

"Law practice, hell. You're a cowman, same as any other Trask."

"Same as Paul?"

Jonathan's lip lifted off his teeth, laughing. "You ain't talking me down. Paul never cottoned to cattle work. You always liked it."

"I like law, too. Look, Buck. You are dead right that Texas has a future. A man can grow with it, but a man follows his bent. As a cowman I would always be a second-rater; in law, even politics some day, I can make some real sense to myself, maybe others too."

Jonathan thought it over and nodded. "Reckon that shines, all right. But whatever you do, you stick close by us, boy, hear me?"

"No argument?"

"Counselor, I'm that downwind of my own plans that I tell you here and now, you got your best customer already. Me. Plain enough I'll need a good head about me to handle legal and business points till I catch up on a lot of learning. And I will, along with the boys. Meantime you can be sizing your other prospects, but all I'm asking, don't jump in all at once."

"I'd planned on staying close to the home awhile anyhow, if it was all the same."

"Good. That's settled." Jonathan lifted in his stirrups and shaded his eyes, peering across the sedgegrass. "God damn. Don't tell me, now. Well, the word has got to be passed and here's a good place to start."

Abruptly he reined on toward a hillcrest. Alex was

puzzled for moments only; now he saw the ribbon of smoke trickling skyward and, as they ranged on across the hill, the brand fire down in a brushy swale, a tied calf and a lone man slapping iron on it. The calf bawled as hair and flesh seared; the squatting man freed the animal before casually lifting his eyes to the pair of riders coming off the slope. Only when they drew rein a few yards off did he rise from his haunches, at the same time tossing the branding iron from his right hand to his left.

Alex was startled by his swift grace, for the man was huge and rawboned. His air of half-caring negligence was deceptive, for his quick movement was purposeful; so was the freeing of his right hand. He wore a .36 Leech and Rigdon in an odd holster that seemed to be riveted swivel-style to his belt. It would be well, always, to watch this man's hand: he could pivot up and fire his gun without clearing leather.

"Buenos dias," he murmured politely, but with his wide clown's smile and big square teeth, several missing, and his tough ugly face, the words were oddly comical.

Jonathan watched him a cold moment, then slowly swung his arm north and south. "You *sabé* the creeks there and there, Pancho, eh?"

"The name, she's Chino Lucero," the big man grinned. A half-shredded *cigarita* projected from a gap in his teeth and he tilted the hot branding iron to light it, screwing up his face like puckered leather. This was comical too, and Alex found himself smiling. "Sure, I know the creeks, and all between them is the Trask land, eh? Sure, man. This is Trask land here, eh?"

"My name is Trask," Jonathan said. "Chew this up and swallow it, Pancho. I'm the big Trask, boy, the one all you brush-popping cow thieves that been living on our beef got to reckon with from here on. I'm serving notice. Anyone gets catched hustling beef on Trask land gets outfitted for a rawhide collar and tall branch. You got any friends, Pancho, you pass the word."

"You are push' pretty damn hard, maybe," Chino Lucero said through his gapped teeth, sleepily smiling. "She is no crime, the branding of plent' loose stuff, eh? My brand is in the county book."

Jonathan lifted his fist and pointed his thumb at Lucero, shaking it gently. "I just made her a crime, Pancho. Cut that calf loose and haze him along. He's the last for you."

He started to swing away, but Lucero called softly, "Hey, Trask. You don't like us, eh, Mexicans?"

"Horse is a horse, greaser's a greaser. I got nothing for the breed one way or other. You got any say, say it."

Lucero slapped the greasy thigh of his *chaparejos*. "Haaah. You think you are big because you are gringo."

"You got it wrong, Pancho. I'm big because I tell you what I'll do, then I will God damn well do it. Just that, *sabé?*"

"You, gringo, who know you?" He snapped his fingers. "You are nobody."

"I will be. I'll have this country in my tote sack before I'm through. Show up at my house by sundown today if you want to work for me. Otherwise I see you on my land again, you're dead."

"Maybe I come," Lucero said with his gap-toothed grin, "to be by when a big rattler like you get stomp' sometime. Haaah."

In the weeks that followed, Alex' unformed plan for a law practice languished and faded into the background as the old free life of the cowhunter claimed him once more. Dawn to dusk he worked and sweated beside the others, feeling his muscles develop from the wrenched soreness of the neophyte to their former hard temper.

During the evenings, by flickering candlelight, he faithfully dredged up effort toward tutoring Jonathan and the two boys. There was a hungry fury to the way Jonathan devoured knowledge; he carried Cort and Liam along on his own dynamic sweep and just as dynamically broke them into his ambitions for the Trask name, letting them frequently side the men in the daily brush-running.

Only Chino Lucero refused to take things very seriously, making a savage game of the whole cowhunting business. A superb rider, full of reckless stunts, absolutely fearless, with an endless capacity for whiskey and women, he saw life as a great joke and lived it accordingly, whether chasing a pretty girl or twisting a *cimaronne's* tail. Yet Jonathan had a gift for bending Chino's primitive, tigerish energies to productive use, and before long the big Mexican was like his extra arm. It was a strange relation, stranger than friendship, between the clowning, irreverent Chino and the grim, iron-eyed man Jonathan Trask was becoming.

Once Jonathan had been much like Chino, but that part of him was eroding away almost as if it had never been. The harder he drove, the more withdrawn and uncommunicative he became. Yet now and again the old Jonathan, with his hearty laugh and rough pranks, would spring out and take you unaware.

When the tally showed two thousand head in the catch, they drove to New Orleans, where Jonathan named and got a cutthroat price for the herd. Afterward he tramped the waterfront, engaging dozens of recently freed and bewildered slaves in talk, sizing each for the qualities he needed to build the toughest, hardest-riding cattle crew the Yegua country had ever seen. They listened with amazement to the big, bearded white man whose words were as hard and sinewy as oak dollops, each one hitting like a club, striking off sparks of manhood and purpose where there had been the apathy of dumb, beaten brutes. Of those asked to hire on, not one refused. Men with women and children were permitted to bring their families, so that it was a black exodus of sorts that followed Jonathan Trask back to Matheson County, Texas.

By now many neighbors had trickled back from the war, men tired and sick and discouraged, flung into deeper gloom by the conditions they found at home. Rounding up and driving the hundreds of wild cattle meant Herculean labors for a meager profit. Jonathan went from one to the next, putting an identical proposition to each: he would round up and drive to Galveston as many trail-broken cattle as they wished sold, dicker the best price available, and turn the entire proceeds over to them. For this service, Jonathan made a novel charge: An acre of land per cow or steer sold on a rancher's behalf. Many scoffed at the suggestion, but a surprising number of disheartened men, caught up by the lure of a new rumored gold strike in California, accepted the offer.

Jonathan promptly set his Negro crew to the task under the blistering tutelage of Chino Lucero, who swore he would make *vaqueros* of each and every one. Jonathan saw that they worked hard, but he left plenty of leeway for them to play just as hard. At the end of each brutal and grinding week, there was a barrel of whiskey waiting; each weekend held a house-raising or two as timber was cut and adzed for sturdy cabins that gradually reduced the squalid tent-camps the families had made along the river.

The circuit rider, Preacher Boggs, was collared one weekend for a camp meeting that lasted three days, during which incredible quantities of food and drink were consumed, nearly twenty souls spoke up for Christ, five unions that had never been maritally blessed became official, and one dozen people were baptized in the Brushy amid a hot debate between Baptists and Methodists over the proper means of the immersion with the Baptist-ordained Mr. Boggs passing a thoroughly partial verdict.

Each night saw an all-night dance where the younger people stomped and swayed barefoot (for shoes would not have survived a single such night) in superb rhythm kept by chanting hand-clappers on the sidelines. It was a wild and beautiful sight that Alex watched for hours on end and never tired of, a highly improvised, life-pulsing promenade somewhere between Africa and hoedown country, with the fireplay of red light on quick lithe bodies and shining black faces.

The third night was climaxed by a bloody dragout brawl over a mulatto girl, Jonathan settling the dispute by having the two participants fight it out with Bowie knives across a handkerchief. However when each had drawn blood, he halted the altercation by rolling out a fresh cask of whiskey and making the two drink each other's health. Within minutes the atmosphere was fiercely convivial, with the whole crew toasting Jonathan, he calling them his gang of crazy God damn burheads and they roaring back at him with affection. Already known throughout the county as "Trask's Niggers," they wore the name as proudly as medals.

Preacher Boggs, a bilious-looking man with a voice like the clarion of judgement, looked on in amazement for a time. Finally he turned to Alex. "Brother McKenna, you know Buck Trask better than anyone outside the Lord that made him. How do you explain him?"

Alex shook his head. "I don't even try, Reverend. I reckon, though, that what really sticks fast in a man's craw when you think on it is that he has just got started."

5

THE TRACK WAS PLAIN: PERHAPS THIRTY HEAD had been driven out of a broad river-bank swale clogged by thorny brazil brush and straggling mesquite, then pushed due eastward along the bank. Jonathan straightened up from examining the track and batted dust from his rawhide *chivarras*. His glance, swinging to Chino Lucero, was as tight and hard as Alex had seen it.

"Third bunch in a week," he said meagerly. "Some of your greaseball friends, you reckon?"

"I'm don't think so." Chino's leathery face crinkled as he squinted an eye nearly shut. "I have tell you a few Mexes have live' off your good Anglo beef time to time, but they poor *peons*, all." He nodded at the tracks. "Boots, not *guarache* track. This was work of *vaqueros*, like me, like you. No greaseballs, I'm think. Only Anglo balls. Haaah."

"Watch your talk about white men," Jonathan growled as he tramped to his horse and stepped into the saddle.

Paul hipped around in his stirrups to ease his hindquarters, remarking dourly, "Now what?" Always an indifferent cattle hand, his missing arm made him more awkward than ever; the grind to which Jonathan had put them all in these last months had told severely on him. Paul had shed weight till he was narrow as a plant, and lines of bitter distaste had etched permanently into his face.

"This time we follow 'em up," Jonathan said flatly, "if it takes all day and night," and put his horse downcreek, his brother and Lucero and Alex following.

This was a fresh step in Jonathan's harsh campaign against the seedy handful of cow thieves, American and Mexican, who had foraged carelessly on Trask range through the war. One by one, Jonathan had caught them out and passed his word: any man who was warned once and afterward mavericked on Buck Trask's land would become free game in an open field. Such men were for the most part poor ne'er-do-wells living on one-loop shoestrings with tribes of slatternly wives and small dirty children. The Mexicans had always been here; the Anglos were second-generation trash from the Southern hills. They knew the Trasks of old; they recalled a younger, dynamic Gideon Trask who had been no man to trifle with, and this son of his was his spit'n'image with something added. So far not a one had not wilted like a pricked balloon before Jonathan's casual iron. He was making no threat, only a simple statement of fact, and they knew it.

Alex' first reading of the change in Jonathan had proved out in a year's time. The press and ambition had swept the dust of residual habit from Jonathan's new bedrock. *Don't tread on me,* the bleakness of his eyes and gaunt set of his shoulders seemed to say. *But you can't be that sure,* Alex told himself. *He drives hard, but for a reason always, and I haven't seen him push a man past his depth. Hard on to his breaking point sometimes, and sometimes a man could hate his guts for that, but never past it. None of them do hate him, though—not a man but wouldn't die for him.*

Yet the table stakes were climbing steadily, trying Jonathan's temper harder. By unhesitatingly seizing his opportunities, Jonathan by a bold swift stroke had bought enough land from his disheartened neighbors to more than quadruple his original holdings. *The land:* this seemed to emerge as the key to his vaulting ambition. Men and women were straws in the wind; when they failed to measure up, to what could a man give his confidence but the earth itself which, being neither faithful nor faithless, was dependable forever?

Downstream within a half mile, the creek broadened and quickened to flat sandy shallows broken by the pale fingers of long sandbars with hoofmarks. Without hesitation, Jonathan led the way across, afterward plunging into the liveoak thickets where the broken passage of cattle lay plain. Now they had left Trask land and were moving straight south; but Jonathan's action made clear that from here on, no mavericker's license or boundary line would protect the one who preyed on his cattle.

Presently the brush began to thin away and they dipped onto a stretch of raw sandhills. Ahead now the dust raised by moving cattle made a tawny shroud; the shouts of the three riders, two point and a drag, drifted clearly.

Jonathan reined up, lifting his hands. "All right, hold up. We will move in slow and then fast; just follow my lead. Chino, take the man on right point. I'll take left." His gaze touched Alex and Paul, and grew faintly sardonic. "Reckon the pair of you can handle that drag man?"

Alex' temper prickled, and prompted rebuttal: "Unless you want help with a point man."

The sun-wrinkles edging Jonathan's eyes crinkled with the small humor rarely seen these days. "All right, then. No shooting unless they offer to start it, *sabé?*"

They broke apart and rode on through the increasing dust; it boiled up in thick billows, obscuring the cattle and riders. Alex tugged up his bandanna around his nose and slipped out his Navy gun. He saw the lean shape of the drag man through the dust and, off to his right, Jonathan's sweeping arm-signal as he broke into a run. Touching spurs lightly, Alex came up at a swift lope behind the drag man. Above the sounds of cattle on the move, the rider heard him and wheeled his mount, clawing at his pistol. Alex fired about his head, the shot heeling across a rattle of gunfire from the right flank where Jonathan was.

"Pull up there," Alex said, "and throw your gun away, left hand." His voice was tense with expecting the shots to stir up the cattle, but they were sluggish and heavy-moving, full of summer grass, and already were idly milling to a stop.

The rider stared at Alex with bitter yellow eyes. He was a long bony man with a pinched and predatory face; Alex had seen others of the breed, shiftless and hog-dirty and footloose transplants of a still older frontier that was vaguely Southern. Wordlessly he lifted out his gun and let it fall to the ground.

The moiling dust began to settle, and Jonathan was moving this way with a dark-faced *vaquero* in tow. The Mexican was gripping a bloody right arm and pouring out fluid profanity.

The bony man called him Diego and told him to shut up. He did, and Jonathan looked hard at the bony man. "What's your name?"

"Creech."

Jonathan swung toward Chino Lucero, who now came up herding a slat-lean youth with hair like grimy straw. He looked like a feeble-headed relation of the bony man. Jonathan said, "Know any of them?"

Chino cocked shut one eye comically. "I'm not know them."

"How about the Mex?"

"Not him neither." Chino grinned. "What you think, I'm knowing.cow thief?"

"You're damned right. How would you size 'em? Ain't ordinary cow thieves from the look, handy-worn guns and all."

"*Vaqueros,* them," Chino agreed. "They all new around. *Muy mal hombres.* Not so bad as you are, but pretty bad."

Jonathan glanced at Paul. "Be useful once, boy, and look over this stuff. See if there's any GT brands in the lot."

Paul pushed through the herd inspecting their flanks, and soon called, "Here's one."

"That's enough," Jonathan said. "Well, Creech, you have trespassed the hell out of my property and taken branded stock."

Creech, yellow-eyed and cautious, hesitated. "One or two brands taken by accident don't make a man a rustler."

"Boy, till now I only passed the word, but it's had time to get around. You must be pretty strange around here. Chuck your guns and light down."

The dirty blond youth shook his head in a slow and positive way. "Not me. I ain't giving up my gun nowise."

"Slack off, Kamas," Creech said. "You'll suit yourself, mister, but this ain't smart."

The blond youth's face tightened with a mounting stubbornness. "I ain't a-going on foot, Jim."

He pawed wildly at his gun, and Jonathan brought his Navy Colt level and pulled trigger. The cap misfired, and Kamas' weapon was swinging up to bear. Almost too fast for the eye to follow, Chino Lucero moved; his Leech and Rigdon swiveled up without leaving his holster. At the flat bellow of the shot, Kamas was rocked sideways out of his saddle. His horse spooked into a gyrating plunge, but the drag of Kamas' dead weight, his foot hung in the stirrup, made the animal settle down.

Creech dropped to the ground; he kept his voice mild. "He was my cousin. We was damn close."

"I don't mean to keep you apart." Jonathan began to tug loose his coiled lariat, and Alex pulled over to his stirrup. "Wait a minute. Is that what you had in mind all the while?"

"What did you figure?"

"That you would warn 'em and set 'em afoot at the most. I thought when you said no shooting—"

"That's because I mean to hang 'em."

Again the Mexican began to chatter volubly, and again Creech told him in a disgusted and savage tone, "Shut up!" He looked at Jonathan, his manner toughening to a bitter contempt. "Go ahead. I said you wasn't smart. When Mr. Danziger—"

"Who's he?"

But Creech said no more. Jonathan dismounted, as did the others except for the terrified Mexican. "Hah, the brave countryman," Chino said, and dragged him to the ground.

Jonathan ordered, "Tie their hands." He settled a veiled stare on Paul. "Scout over by the crick and locate a sound limb."

Alex sidled off from the others a little. He still had a thin hope Jonathan might be bluffing, but he wanted to be in a position to get the drop if there were no other way to stop it.

Paul, white around the lips, shook his head. "There's law to cover this. I won't be a party."

"Law," Jonathan snorted softly. "That might be what ails the counselor—not you. A man with no belly for man's work should stay where the women are." He suddenly tilted his Navy Colt enough to loosely cover

Alex. "Don't move around like that, counselor."
Something in his face made the sweat start on Alex'
belly, and he thought, *Now you know.*

"Buck, don't. It's like Paul said."

"Don't figure I can get away with it?"

"Not the point. Given the conditions, people can get
away with a good deal. The point is, you're wrong."

"Who's wrong?" Jonathan's tone was flinty with
self-certainty. "You're wrong? Your fancy-ass court's
wrong?" He tapped his chest. "Out here, there's
nothing but me. I can name any right, any wrong,
because I got the power to make it stick. Ain't nothing
else that counts."

"Where did your license to decide life and death
begin?"

"Right here." Jonathan ground his heel into the dun
earth. "I could let off them petty bummers and thieves
that was scavenging off us before. I knew that they was
and how they could be scared away. A word here and
there done it. If there'd been need for more, don't
think I would of drawn any line. This's different. You
heard how me and Chino size these fellows. You heard
this Creech name somebody. This is an operation, a
leader and all. I don't know what it means, but I'll find
out. The whole country knows my word on rustling, so
this had to be a test. All right. I aim to see they don't
read me amiss. There's just one answer they can't
mistake."

They rode along the upper creek to a line of spindly
cottonwoods. Jonathan chose one with a thick limb of
convenient height. He and Chino slung their ropes
across the limb; Chino's falling noose grazed the
Mexican rustler's face and he jerked his head away and
began screaming.

Chino said in Spanish, "Be still, boy, you disgrace

us," and gave him a cuff across the cheek. The shock of the blow, not the words, silenced the Mexican; he sat shaking, mumbling, as Chino adjusted the noose.

Creech sat still-faced, but he was sweating. "Look. Maybe we can talk about paying you for them."

"Talk all you want," Jonathan said. "You'll pay all right." He slipped the noose over Creech's head and kneed his horse around behind them. He lashed at the speckled rump of the Mexican's horse and it walked away, letting the man's full weight drop and swing. He kicked and writhed and slowly strangled. Jonathan struck at Creech's horse; when it didn't move he swore and struck again. The rope was new, the loop around Creech's neck stiff and loose. Creech, with a vigorous twist of his head, freed himself as the horse stepped forward. He slammed home his spurs and drove his horse into a run.

Jonathan snapped at Chino, "Drop him," and the big man took his time, bringing his gun up and spacing his shots. Creech streaked for the nearest thickets bent low in his saddle; not a bullet touched him. Jonathan cursed and rammed his pistol into his belt, reaching for his Sharps in its scabbard. His aim was swift and careful. He fired just as Creech attained the fringe of the thicket. The horse made a limp, bouncing roll across the rocky ground and was motionless.

Jonathan lowered his rifle. "Why didn't you get him first shot, Mex?"

"Maybe I don' like putting it in a man's back, eh?" Chino grinned and shrugged vastly. "Haaah. Maybe I want to see how you do once."

"You know now. Mex, don't ever again miss that way when you got an order."

Paul was dropping off his horse and then, on his

knees, he vomited. Jonathan did not even glance at him. He motioned with his rifle at the two dead men, Creech and the blond. "We'll string them both up along with the greaseball. Leave 'em hang. They got friends will find 'em when they don't show up, and I want my sign clear to every one of them cow-lifting bastards."

6

KATYTOWN, WHICH GIDEON TRASK AND OTHER settlers had started to develop in 1848 with a crossroads store, had changed little since the war. They had named it by mixing their wives' names on slips of paper in Jim Killgrew's old beaver and drawing, Vad Bristow's Katherine being the winner. Within five years the site boasted a couple of dozen homes, a blacksmith shop, Baptist and Methodist churches, two general merchandise stores, a wagon yard and livery stable, a drugstore run by a licensed physician, and a go-for-the-gut Secesh newspaper. Except for a new flour mill and a growing set of oaks and sycamores along the street, it hadn't changed a lot. Alex liked the town and had once hoped to set up law practice here, but he liked progress too.

This bright Saturday morning, riding in with all the Trasks on the monthly hegira to take care of marketing and minor bits of business, he felt the usual dim touch of guilt. A short year ago he'd returned to Texas full of personal hopes and plans. He loved range life, but the fact remained he'd let at least a modest destiny trickle away from him, along with the use of a mind and talent that fitted him for more than cattle work.

Still the Trasks needed him; he was the friend who mortared together the loose stones of their too-exclusive selves. His presence did undeniably ease the various strains created by Jonathan's ambition, Mercy's weakness for him, Paul's morbid complexes, old Gideon's senility and Cort's wildness and Liam's dim independence.

As they jogged into Katytown, Cort and Liam were leading the rustlers' horses, full gear on their backs. Alex had urged Jonathan to turn over the horses, guns and gear of the three men to the sheriff and tell him everything as it had happened. If charges were brought against him, his initiative in bringing the matter before the law would help his defense. Having made his point by the triple hanging, Jonathan had no objection.

They threaded the mild currents of Saturday traffic with hellos to acquaintances and "neighbors," and slipped their horses and wagons into a vacant place at the rail flanking the courthouse. This was a long frame building with a fieldstone basement where the sheriff had his dank cubicle of an office.

The men stepped off their horses, except for Gideon Trask, who got stiffly down off the wagon seat he had shared with Mercy.

During the past year, Gideon had made something of a comeback. Seeing Jonathan's stiff-handed taking over of the enterprises he'd begun had made him button-popping proud. But the new Gideon was ages removed from the old; once stern and reserved, he'd become a garrulous crony of ne'er-do-wells, bragging up Jonathan incessantly. He'd continued his heavy drinking and there was a childish quality to the way he now followed his son's lead.

Jonathan reached up and clasped his hand to Mercy's waist, and swung her down from the wagon. The gesture was almost suggestive in its easy familiarity and Mercy, as her feet touched the ground, drew quickly back, flushed. A hint of casual affection between in-laws shouldn't have seemed particularly offshade, but Jonathan had made the proprietory gesture with a kind of purposive deliberation that brought the heavy blood crawling into Paul's face.

Jonathan was already swinging away; he said, "Do what you-all want; it's a holiday." He slapped Alex on the arm. "We'll see Mapin right off."

Cort moved around his horse, an old Paterson Model Colt that had been his father's strapped to his thigh. He imitated Jonathan's walk, a solid and slightly rolling gait that went with his older brother's bulk but with Cort's wiry frame was mildly ludicrous. Still you didn't feel like laughing. Liam, his dark eyes timid and furtive as he looked about, held close beside Cort.

"Needing me, Buck?"

"No. Here." Jonathan dug out a pair of coppers. "Get some horehounds."

Cort said softly, "I ain't no kid, Buck. I ain't big like you was at sixteen, but I outgrowed candy." His eyes were hot with resentment.

"Did you?" Jonathan said with his heavy-handed irony. "Never did, myself." He flipped the coins to Liam. "Here you, Li, get some for us all."

As he and Jonathan went into the store and down a rickety stairs, Alex remarked, "You ought to take that thing away from him."

"Who? What?"

"Cort. The gun."

"Jesus," Jonathan said. "I'd swear you never come back from the East. Got to outfit like a man to make a man. Here a man ain't dressed without a gun."

"I don't argue that, but the outfit doesn't make the man."

Jonathan halted at the bottom of the stairs, his look grim and quizzical in the basement gloom. "You think he's growing up too fast?"

Alex shook his head. "You know better. In Texas you can't grow up too fast. I've no idea what sort of man

Cort might grow into otherwise, but he'll never be your kind, Buck." He paused, and Jonathan said nothing, grimly waiting. "He's trying to follow you, Buck, and he'll never cut it. Cort has your ambition and your temper without your strength or your way with men. As for his judgment, he has none to speak of, not even as sorry as yours."

Jonathan's face darkened; his right fist lifted a bare inch, then settled and unclenched. "No man under the sun but you could say that to me, boy. No man."

Alex only nodded, and then Jonathan wheeled and led off down a moldy corridor to the room at its end. Sheriff Mapin, a string bean of a man with a long and mournful face, was at his rolltop desk reading the county mail. After an exchange of greetings, Jonathan sat down on a creaking crate which, upended by the desk, served as a visitor's chair. "Lou, you ain't been out our way in a coon's age."

Mapin said, "It's a big country, Buck," but Alex, folding his arms as he leaned his back against a damp wall, knew that Mapin never outdid himself in making the rounds of his territory. He listened without expression till Jonathan had told his story.

"Well"—Mapin took out a pocket knife, opened the small blade and began paring his nails, frowning—"that was playing hell, you know, Buck. I don't blame you none, though ever'body and his uncle is picking unbranded strays out of the brush—"

"Not on Trask land they ain't. There was branded stuff mixed in, and I don't call that kind of drive-off any picking up strays."

"Don't either. Point is"—Mapin expertly flicked off a hangnail with the razor tip of his blade—"you should of hung the bastards and kept quiet, particularly to me. Law's law Buck. If you wanted to go after 'em off your own land and let the law know, should of come to me and I'd of deputized you to bring 'em in. Could be dead or alive, I wouldn't much care." He sighed gently, closing the blade. "Only now you'll be standing trial."

"Good," Jonathan said grimly. "I want the whole country to make my sign out clear. Give me a cowman's jury and I'll tell you the verdict now." He veered the subject. "Lou, there's more to this than three out-at-the-heels bummers picking up a few odd cows. It was the whole look of things. You know anything at all about 'em, Creech or that Kamas or the Mex?"

Mapin scratched his chin. "Nothing but their names and how they look. They'd be James Creech and Kamas Mobley and Diego Montoya. Couldn't of told you that much before a month ago. That's when they started coming to Katytown, them and some others. Drift in and out a few at a time, but the way you see different ones together, clear they're all tied in. Upwards of a dozen or so, and a hard crew. This one big fellow seems to be the leader. Man named Danziger."

"Creech said the name."

"Has a funny first name like a woman's, Alice or Alvina. I rec'lect—Alvah. Word has it he was with them Redlegs and Jayhawkers up in Missouri in the war."

"Guerrillas," Jonathan said tersely. "What else you know, Lou?"

"Ever hear of the Notchcutters?"

Jonathan and Alex exchanged glances. The Notchcutters were a loose federation of cow- and horse-thief gangs who had preyed on the Texas cattlemen for years. Since the war's end, their operations had become swollen and sprawling as their ranks were augmented by deserters and scalawags, the flotsam of both armies. It was rumored that they had friends among state legislators and local officials in various county seats, men who quietly fattened in their service by twisting the law to criminal advantage. Men who had simply defended their rights as citizens had been framed and jailed on the flimsiest of charges. The Notchcutters took their name from a dangerous but proudly flaunted habit of carving a notch on their gunstocks for each murdered victim.

Jonathan said only, meagerly, "We brought in the horses of the ones we hung, all their possibles too. You'll find the pistol grips hacked up some."

"Same with the live ones," Mapin said. "This Alvah Danziger is likely one of their top men. Looks like a big dirty hog, dresses like one too, but is a schooled man and wellspoken. Appears they've pushed operations into Matheson County and Danziger is sort of the district manager." He hesitated. "They approached me and Judge Sharpe. Likewise Williamson, the new county attorney. I can answer for me and the judge, but won't be sure how Williamson stands till a Notchcutter gets brought to trial."

"Hell's blood," Jonathan snapped. "Why ain't you bringing 'em in, Lou?"

Mapin gave a faint, wry shrug. "You're the first they hit, Buck. First that's complained, anyway. And you took your own step." He paused thoughtfully. "Means now they've sized things up, they're starting their moves."

They talked things over with Mapin awhile longer, then took their leave. Jonathan was scowling and thoughtful. The harsh justice he'd dealt to three of the gang would have about as much effect on their total operation as a handful of snow on a prairie fire.

"Where to?" Alex said.

"Blacksmith's," Jonathan growled. He slipped his Navy Colt from its homemade holster and broke out the cylinder. "This thing misfired on me yesterday. Time I had her converted for metal cartridges."

They crossed the street to Judd Farnum's smithy. Alex, unfamiliar with the new metallic shells, listened with interest as Farnum explained how he converted percussion-cap pistols to fire cartridges. With the old percussion guns you had to load each chamber with powder and ball; then you primed the nipple located behind each chamber with percussion caps. The hammer hitting a cap caused fire to flash through an access hole to the powder in the chamber. What Farnum did was shear off the rear of the cylinder along with the nipples and affix a disc with holes to insert the one-unit cartridges containing primer and powder and bullet in the chamber. He also modified the hammer by adding a firing pin to hit the cartridge primers. "Seems everybody's bringing in their guns to be fixed over," Farnum observed. "I'm getting a mighty sure hand for the job."

"That's good," Jonathan said. "You can have it ready by four this afternoon."

"Well, there's all kinds of jobs ahead of—"

"Four," Jonathan said. "This afternoon."

He watched Farnum's eyes as he spoke, and Farnum, as big a man as Jonathan, shifted his gaze to the forge. "Sure." He spat delicately. "All right."

As they left the smith shop, Alex reflected that the men Jonathan put down could be weak or strong; it was all the same. They might look equal to dealing with him; somehow they never were.

Jonathan halted and took out a cold cigar, half-smoked; he mouthed it with a wry look and struck a match on his heel, shaking off a sulphurous flare of sparks before holding it to his cigar. "See what Lou meant?" He motioned along the street. "More'n a few strange ones in town."

Alex saw him stiffen, and followed his glance. Mercy was proceeding down the street, her arms full of packages, and a bearded, dirty-looking man was weav-

ing toward her. He was drunk. Jonathan flung away his
cigar and moved forward, but too late. The drunk
collided with Mercy hard enough to spin her lightly
against a wall, knocking all the packages to the ground.

. A dozen running steps and Jonathan was on the man;
he caught him by the collar and whirled him, driving his
big fist into the middle of his face. The man skidded on
his rear in the dust; lying there, he shook his head,
drew the back of a hairy hand across his broken lips,
and then started for his gun. Jonathan took a long
stride and another, and on the second one, let his boot
sweep on in a savage arc that caught the bearded man's
wrist as he brought up the gun.

Alex heard the bitter crack of bone breaking; the
man shrieked.

"That's enough!"

Alex, hurrying after Jonathan, came to a stop as the
words whipped out. He saw a tall man braced in the
middle of the street some yards off, hand on his gun. It
was he who'd spoken. He was smiling, but his eyes were
cold as death. He was lean and long and elegant with a
rust-colored mustache; he wore neat range clothes and
was no cowhand.

Alex had never seen a killer before; not a man, that
was, who had killed and gotten a taste for blood and
was ready to kill again. Jonathan was facing the man
fully now, tensing, and Alex wanted to cry, *Don't*, at
him. Then Jonathan, remembering in time, sighed and
slowly straightened his great frame, raising his hands
enough to pull back his coat and show his holster
empty.

The elegant man smiled under his mustache; he even
laughed gracefully, like ice tinkling. Had Jonathan
been armed, Alex knew, he would be dead this
moment.

Standing beside the elegant gunman, a little behind

him, was a great hog of a man in a stained and wrinkled suit. His red hair was matted in a dirty tangle; his several chins sparkled with golden whiskers. His wide bland eyes and the tilted tufts of his brows gave him an air of faint surprise. He moved heavily forward now, saying quietly, "What a pity, Mr. Trask."

Jonathan raked him with a cold glance, said, "Danziger, eh," and nodded down at the groaning man by his feet. "One of yours?"

Mercy, as if out of a mechanical need to do something, stooped and began gathering up her littered packages with trembling hands. Alex moved over to help her, keeping his eyes on the huge, hoglike man.

Alvah Danziger doffed his shapeless rawhide hat with an almost courtly sweep. "My apologies, dear lady"—his voice was warm as summer butter—"for this incident. You've been pointed out to me, sir; your companion, Mr. McKenna, as well. This is my broher, Lat." He indicated the elegant gunman. "Shall we waste words, Mr. Trask? Or, seeing that we went to the trouble to learn one another's identities, shall we consider all's known that needs to be?"

"I never waste words," Jonathan murmured. "Three of your boys found that out." He turned his head and spat across his shoulder toward the hitchrail, at the horses of the hung outlaws. "You want to claim their stuff?"

Alvah Danziger looked carefully at the three horses; his eyes lidded down sleepily. "Three of my associates had been missing. I'd wondered, till we found their bodies. Dear me, you're a forceful young man. We'd merely been engaged in branding wild steers."

"Meaning any and all, mine included."

"Is that why you murdered my poor friends? You've left me no choice but to request a warrant sworn out for your arrest on their behalf."

Jonathan stared at him. "You've got your gall, by God!"

"Not really, sir. Murder is murder, even if you can show that a few animals wearing your brand were accidentally picked up by Messrs. Creech, Mobley, and Montoya. Lat, see our friend with the injured wrist to a physician, would you? Good day to you, gentlemen, and you, ma'am. I must build a small fire under Mr. Mapin."

7

AN HOUR LATER SHERIFF MAPIN, NOT A LITTLE
embarrassed, handed Jonathan a warrant for the
murders of James Creech and Diego Montoya. He also
had a warrant for Chino Lucero, who had shot Kamas
Mobley.

"Ain't no hurry," Mapin said. "I'll fetch it out to
your place tomorrow or sometime."

"Hope there's no notion afoot of holding us till
trial," Jonathan said ominiously.

"Hell, no, not even with bail. Judge Sharpe knows
cowfolks in these parts well enough to bend the book
when need be. A man's work don't take care of itself.
I'll fetch word when your trial is set, and you come in
for it."

Late that afternoon, promptly after Jonathan had
picked up his converted pistol at the smith's, the Trasks
and Alex headed back for the GT, the wagon bed
heaped with supplies. Jonathan rode in a kind of grim
brooding, shredding a cigar between his teeth, humili-
ated by being jostled into a legally defensive position by
a thief and scalawag like Alvah Danziger.

"Well, lawyer. Suppose this puts a tally on your
string."

"Let's say that what's happened hasn't made me
wrong."

Jonathan shuttled a grim glance at him. "How would you a-stopped that dumb boy, Kamas, when he throwed down, chucked a lawbook at him?"

"How will you stop Danziger in court?" Alex countered. "The law hereabouts would have looked the other way for your hanging those rustlers, but with Danziger making himself the local gadfly, the matter won't be left to simmer down. Everything I've heard indicates he's already gained the county attorney's loyalty. He's no ordinary cow thief, Buck. Just a gun or a noose can't stop him."

"Stopping him in court's your job. Chew it hard."

Alex did considerable chewing well into that afternoon, when he and the Trask brothers and some of the Negro hands were engaged in building new gather pens for the upcoming cow hunt. Hardwoods from downstream were being felled and trimmed, cut into lengths, and conveyed by post wagon to the prairie flats north of the ranch layout. The posts were sunk three feet in the earth and lashed together with strips of green cowhide, forming corrals that experience had shown would restrain the fiercest and most powerful longhorns. Theirs was a one-outfit team now; the GT had become too big to make its cow hunts a neighborly operation. So Jonathan had ruled, and made his word firm by having the new hunt pens constructed on home ground.

Toward midafternoon, as he and Paul were driving the post wagon back from the groves with a fresh load of trimmed lengths, Alex snapped his fingers. "Might be," he murmured. "It just might."

"What?" Paul asked.

"A way for us to handle Danziger brothers and company." They were nearly to the new pens, and shading his eyes, Alex saw a man leaving the work detail, heading for the house across the flats. He was carrying a couple of buckets. "That's Buck . . . looks like he's going for water. Well, he'll want to hear my idea right away."

Alex dropped off the wagon when they halted by the pens, then left the others to unload and headed for the house at a saunter, still thinking over his idea and pleased as a boy with it. He came up along the flank of the house to reach the well at the back where Jonathan would be filling the buckets. The half-absent thought came to him that water-toting was the sort of chore Jonathan would ordinarily leave to one of the boys, Cort or Li.

Perhaps the thought gave a wary jog to his preoccupation; at any rate he came to a dead stop as a low drift of voices came to him from around the corner of the house. Mercy's voice, and Jonathan's. They were talking over by the well.

"I wish you wouldn't," Mercy was saying unhappily. "Stealing back here like this to see me."

"Seeing you is all I asked for so far," came Jonathan's deep mutter. "I'm getting might short-strung with just seeing."

"You mustn't, oh you mustn't," she was almost crying. "I'm trying to make Paul a good wife—"

"Sure you are," he said with bitterness. "You was mine first, Mercy, and no preacher's word can gainsay it. I ain't ever going to feel different on it, not ever. You hear? Not ever!"

The harshness that had grown on him had slipped momentarily; hurt and hunger and a painful yearning were in his voice. Mercy said with a soft, choked misery, "Oh—don't. Find another girl and marry her and let me alone, Jon, please!"

"You're my girl. Won't ever be any other. Mercy!"

"No—no—" There were muffled sounds like a small struggle; Alex let his weight come forward, then settled back on his heels with a dismal futility. The sounds were different now, and he turned and walked back the way he'd come, feeling more sorrow than disgust, more helplessness than anger.

He could not help, he could only hurt by speaking up; he could say nothing to Paul. And trying to sway Jonathan would be worse than useless.

The next day, after a talk with Jonathan, Alex rode to Katytown alone. Enlisting the help of Sheriff Mapin, he spent the next several days asking questions, sifting bits of information, learning all he could about the Danziger brothers and the gang of riffraff that followed them. When he'd thanked Mapin for his help and left town, Alex had a complete list of names of the gang members and all that was known about each one. He returned briefly to the ranch for another consultation with Jonathan, and within a couple of hours was riding away again. This time he was packed for a longer trip and a longer stay.

He returned from Austin two weeks later, tired and worn but wearing a jubilant grin that said things had gone well. Jonathan's and Chino's trial was two days away; by now word had gone around and half the county would be there to witness the first open clash between cowman and organized outlawry. The outcome could determine local politics for years to come, a fact that was seeping strongly home to the citizenry.

From the moment court convened, it was clear that the county attorney, Williamson, was pressing hard for a conviction. Alex scanned the room while Williamson was questioning a prospective juror, noting the many Notchcutters packed among the spectators. Alvah Danzinger was on a rear bench, fanning himself with his hat, stoic as a large toad; his brother Lat slumped loose-jointed beside him, eyes cold and unblinking.

Jonathan had said, "No jury in Texas will convict a man for hanging his own rustlers," but Williamson did a fair job of isolating jurymen that were at least professedly impartial.

When prosecution and defense had made their statements, things moved quickly. Alvah Danziger fanned himself complacently; he appeared corpulently amused by Jonathan's utterly factual and incriminating statement of his action and intent. Chino, it was clear, had fired defensively and would secure an easy acquittal, while Jonathan, it seemed, was miring himself hopelessly in his own straightforwardness.

But through Alex' skilled drawing-out he was doing more; he was making every manjack in the room—or within earshot, since the windows and doorway were crowded with craning spectators—aware of what he had taken on himself and why. He had given an answer for all of them to Danziger and his ilk, an answer they understood and applauded to a man. Literally, for Judge Sharpe had to rap for silence several times to quell bursts of cheering.

Danziger's smile began to stiffen on his cheeks; he fanned himself harder. Whether he won or lost today, an aware public opinion was forming against him. He was watching it harden before his eyes.

Patiently, using what was ostensibly Jonathan's trial, Alex built his case against the Notchcutters. All of Williamson's attempts to quash Alex' line of defense were unsuccessful. His last objection was voiced when Alex introduced a pocket of papers containing evidence on the characters and legal statuses of the men Jonathan had allegedly murdered and requested the court's permission to read it aloud. Judge Sharpe placidly overruled the objection; the court would decide for itself whether the testimony was relevant and would instruct the jury accordingly.

For the next half hour Alex reeled off information on the robber alliance called the Notchcutters, its history, its leaders, its methods. And above all, the kind of men it recruited. He branded the three dead rustlers as killers and thieves of the worst stripe, documented his case exhaustively with the facts he had garnered from the state authorities in Austin. Diego Montoya was wanted in Arizona for breaking jail after being arrested on suspicion of the knife-murders of two women. Jim Creech and Kamas Mobley were wanted in northern counties on different charges of robbery, and Creech was also wanted for murder in Kansas. Alex did not stop there; he went on to state with biting exactness the record of every outlaw in the courtroom. "The jury has a duty," he concluded, "to absolve the man who rid them of three jackals and scavengers who resembled men. They ought to pay him a bounty."

It was thorough and damning, and the jury did not even retire; one phrase rippled from man to man, and the foreman stood up. "Not guilty, y'r honor."

The courtroom erupted with cheering. Alvah Danziger stood ponderously, his face holding a mottled darkness, and shouldered his way back through the crowd toward the door. Lat Danziger, moving behind him, gave brief nods right and left, signaling the others. The Notchcutters detached themselves from the crowd and filed out after their leaders.

Jonathan, grinning, clapped his arm solidly across Alex' shoulders. "Come on. I want to read my sign to Brother Danziger before he leaves town."

The two of them pushed out past the crowd and went to the long hitchrail at the side. Danziger's men were mounted, and the big man was heaving his own bulk into saddle; he danced his short-coupled brute around in a tight arc, then held it in as he saw the two of them approaching.

"Most thorough of you, Mr. McKenna. But a legal victory is not a military one, Mr. Trask; a skirmish is not the war."

Jonathan's big hands spraddled his hips; his beard was jutting. "That's all right. I won't be fighting with my hands tied, like you hoped. If I can catch and hang three curly wolves, I can hang twelve. Or a hundred. The law just said so. Cut your wolves loose, fat man, or run for your holes."

Danziger nodded slowly, gently. "We'll run—for now. After Mr. McKenna's moving statement in the courtroom, I shouldn't want to take on your whole county."

"You don't need to worry about the county, fat man," Jonathan said grinning. "All you got to worry about is me, because I'll be enough. You got to walk over me first, and you won't never make it."

Danziger's wattles shook; the mottled anger deepened in his face, and he flung his horse half-around and rode away with his men.

Alvah Danziger was true to his word. For a week nothing happened, but meantime it was noted by Katytown citizens that Danziger's crowd was purchasing huge stores of grub supplies, buying up in one swoop all the cases of new metal cartridges stocked at Old Montrose's store.

Jonathan learned as much when he tried to buy a supply for his crew. He'd given his men orders to have their old sidearms converted or to acquire one of the new Smith and Wesson revolvers made for jacketed shells. Seething and worried, he doled out to the crew from his own cartridges.

Alvah Danziger hadn't been seen since the day of the trial, and abruptly, as if their plans were laid, their supplies safely cached, all his men ceased to show themselves. It was the signal for a thieves' offensive that spared the cattle and horse stock of no ranch in three counties. They hit according to the tactics Danziger and his kind had perfected during the war, making swift, small night raids in a dozen different places in lightning success throughout Lee, Matheson, and Bastrop counties.

A substantial loss was often not discovered for several days, and once trackers picked up the sign, they could rarely follow it far. The thieves clung to watercourses and thickly brushed areas where trailing was next to impossible. They made quick, break-up camps, changing the sites every few days. The Austin newspapers warned travelers to hold to open country and avoid trails through trees and thickets. A man could never tell when or where he might ride into the guns of encamped killers; those who did never lived to describe the meetings. . . .

Repeatedly Jonathan set up ambushes at different spots along the thicket-matted banks of the Yegua and Brushy creeks. They made contact with thieves only twice, and on both occasions the quarry got clean away in the dark. It was like boxing with shadows, while the Pig (as Jonathan had dubbed Danziger) bled the range of three counties of the stock that was life itself to people who had made a slow, grueling comeback from the war years, only to find their hard-won gains being nibbled away. Something had to be done, and soon.

One morning Jonathan called Alex into his office. Paul was already there, seated at the desk and looking blankly at an open ledger. Chino had also been summoned; he sat on the edge of the desk, swinging a spurred foot. Jonathan shut the door behind Alex, then settled his shoulders against the wall and lighted a cigar.

"We're in trouble," he said without preliminary. "The pinch is getting bad, and we're riding on credit. Too many irons in the fire."

Alex, who handled the ranch bookkeeping, said with a trace of irritation, "Well, I warned you long before this trouble started about tying up all your money. By now even your credit is getting tight."

Jonathan pinched out his match. "These thieving bastards got to be stopped. Dead. Now."

"That's fine," Alex said. "You can't even dig out this rumored 'underground' system whereby they're supposed to be moving the stolen stuff in night drives down to the crooked Gulf Coast buyers. And nothing else has worked."

"God damn it—" Jonathan pushed away from the wall, scowling. "Don't tell me again what ain't worked. Put your heads into it. Show me an idea. Kick it around."

Nobody said anything for a minute, and then Paul ventured, "If we knew for sure where they were going to hit once and just when and how, we could lay an ambush so smart they couldn't wriggle out."

Jonathan gave him a disdainful stare. "Just two things wrong with that. We got no way of telling for sure where or when and if we did have, we wouldn't net more'n three or four and likely not Danziger at all. We got to get the lot, and we got to smoke out the Pig."

Paul's thin fingers turned white gripping a pen. "Don't ride me, Buck. You wanted ideas; we have to start somewhere."

"If we had something going," Alex put it quickly, "something big enough to toll the whole crew into the openwell, say a cow hunt to end all hunts. A lot of cows together make a big target. One nobody would try for with just a handful of men."

"*If* they tried for it," Jonathan growled, then snapped his fingers and wheeled toward Chino. "Mex—!"

Chino said, "I'm listen', man," as he finished building a shuck cigarette and inserted it in a corner of his grin.

"You said once you thought these Notchcutters might of made a few friends hereabouts. Was that a windy, or do you know something?"

Chino had taken out his steel *eslabón* and tinder cord; now his hands grew still. "Maybe," he said guardedly.

"If you're working for me, don't maybe me, boy. Be sure."

Chino began idly striking sparks into the tinder with his *eslabón*, and he said finally, "There is a cousin of mine. I ain' tell you his name. I think maybe he know som'thing. I don' think he's in it, but he knows some who been helping them an' how they are doing things."

"God damn," Jonathan said wickedly, and leaned almost into Chino's face. "You been holding out on me?"

"Ain' that." Chino was utterly calm; he lodged a spark in the tinder and blew it into flame, then held it to his cigarette. "Might make my cousin trouble to say som'thing. I don' have that, Trask."

Chino had his own peculiar brand of respect for Jonathan, but he was not afraid of him; Chino feared nothing alive. He took insults and gibes lightly, shrugging them aside with inexhaustible humor, but beyond a point nobody prodded him.

Jonathan teetered back on his heels, nodding. "Well, Mex, there won't be no trouble for your cousin. Don't even care what his name is. What I'm asking, could you get him to help us?"

"Haaah." Chino displayed his gap-toothed amusement. "For why, hah? Why you think he should help you?"

"For money."

Chino's hand, returning his cigarette to his lips, made a mild shrugging gesture. "Maybe—for money. She's all depend on what you want."

"I'll tell you," Jonathan growled. "Pay attention now."

8

TWO DAYS LATER CHINO REPORTED THAT HIS cousin was willing to pass along all he could learn about the Notchcutter activities. He would do this for two hundred dollars. "And considerations," Chino added, winking at Alex, "like the lawyer fella say. Haaah." Jonathan wanted to know what considerations. "When you round up these *ladrones* he don' want to get picked up too," Chino explained. "And the two hundred, she must be in gold."

With a spy in the enemy camp making regular reports through Chino, Jonathan went ahead with the rest of the plan based on Alex' suggestion. The cow hunt, the biggest the county had ever seen, began the next day.

The enlarged Trask pens, stout postoak fences secured together by iron-hard rawhide lacings, now covered twenty acres. Headed by Malachi, Jonathan's big Negro *segundo,* a *corrida* of thirty men worked out through the dense mesquite and chaparral that cloaked the bottomlands.

Jonathan's new-fangled branding traps, the first in the region, enabled them to brand with three times the speed and ease of the old rope and throw method. In a short time the pens were loaded to capacity with road-branded and somewhat gentled cattle.

The Notchcutters had still made no move, and their

informant had nothing to report yet. Chino meagerly revealed that his cousin had ingratiated himself into the circle of rustlers, proving himself by accompanying them on several raids, but neither he nor any of the minor outlaws had the confidence of the leaders and he couldn't tell exactly what was brewing.

"Got to carry through," Jonathan said. "Hadn't planned to ship so many cows this spring with all them Kansas and Missouri sodgrubbers bitching about that fever they say we been spreading to their stock. Be lucky to get any through without shootings and stampedes. But we got the cows and we can't send 'em all to the hide and tallow plants. Can't turn 'em loose now without the Pig knowing we was setting up a target for him."

"What's the difference," Paul said, "if he don't make a move?"

"Difference is, we hold out a mite longer and he might just move yet. I allow he's suspicious and careful; so far he's made these little strikes. If we get the cattle moving north, a big herd on the move might toll the Pig out of hiding."

"Way too many for a herd."

"Not for two herds. Start 'em out a day or two apart. If we don't push 'em no farther'n Baxter Springs, Kansas, we might not even run afoul them farmers."

"There's no shipping facilities at Baxter Springs," Alex pointed out.

"Well, a whole lot of trouble has been them God damn freesoilers purely hate Texans. I figure we can dicker a fair price out of a Yankee buyer who's willing to gamble he can move 'em over the fort road to Kansas City or St. Joe."

The first herd started out the next day, Jonathan trail-bossing. Malachi was to start the second herd moving in two days. Each herd contained three thousand head, the maximum Jonathan considered safe; other cowmen gave arguments favoring both sides of that figure. Fifteen riders to each herd, with the cook and his roustabout driving the two *carretas* piled with grub and the crew's gear. Alex, along with Gideon Trask and Paul, accompanied the first herd. Chino was to remain at the ranch to receive any information relayed by his cousin; if anything developed, he was to carry word to Jonathan as fast as horseflesh would take him.

A few days later, south of Belton, where Jonathan planned to swing onto Jesse Chisholm's trade road, Chino caught up with the first herd. His horse was blowing and lathered, and the big Mexican was reeling with exhaustion. They had to lift him out of the saddle, and Jonathan produced a bottle of whiskey from the cook's stores.

"That's medicinal, Mex," he warned. "One jolt to prime your pump, then you talk."

"Haaah," Chino said, and drank deeply. "The word is out to the crowd, my little cousin say. All of them, they will meet together and ride north. They will hit this big herd tomorrow night. They will drive off what they can, but mostly the Peeg, he want to ruin you, Trask. So they all are saying, my cousin says. As long as Danziger ruin you, he don' care how many cattle they get. To wreck your drive is what he want."

Jonathan muttered, "Hoped he would," and gave his orders. In minutes the herd was on the move again, and Jonathan pushed hard through that day and well into the night. A halt after dark, grub, nighthawks assigned, and a few hours' sleep. They were out of their blankets at false dawn and had rolled up a full five miles before sunrise broke on the paling prairie.

Jonathan clearly had an objective in mind, but he

confided in nobody, not even his father or Alex. He was hard to talk to, brooding, muttering under his breath; that meant he was stewing out the problem from every angle, and nobody questioned him.

The character of the country was slyly altering, broken now with dry canyons and shallow rises. Soon Jonathan himself moved out on scout; he returned within the hour and ordered a slight swing to the northeast. This might be to detour the herd around impossible terrain, but more likely he was pointing them toward a specific place. That idea was confirmed when, shortly before sunset, they came to the low beetling cliffs called the Cibola Breaks, an upheaval of canyon-cleft ridges that disturbed the prairie running east and west. The cattle could be run through some of the canyon passages, but not without difficulties.

At one point the ridges cupped a broad well-grassed vale shaped like a bottle, with wide canyons offering access at each end. Jonathan had them sweat the whole herd into the large end of this valley before he called a halt, ordering camp pitched in the tapering end of the bottle.

The exhausted men wolfed their food as the washed blue of the prairie sky grew smoky with day's end. The first crewman to finish eating loudly clattered his utensils into the cook's wreckpan, and Jonathan roundly cursed him for it. Sound carried in brittle waves between these walls, and the cattle were edgy from being pushed too hard. Alex ate with the three Trasks. As they were drinking their coffee, squatting on their haunches, Jonathan broke silence at last:

"If they hit us tonight, they got to hit us where they find us. I want 'em to find us here."

"That's clear enough, but why here?" Alex made a wide circle with his hand. "We're in the open, surrounded by ridges. We'd be cold meat if men got above us with rifles. They could pin us on all sides while they cut us to pieces."

"Oh," Paul said half-viciously, flinging out his coffee dregs. "Our leader wouldn't overlook a little thing like that."

Jonathan nodded gently, almost sleepily. "That's what'll happen, but not to us. We'll be the ones up there. Waiting for the Pig and his friends to get under our guns."

Alex said skeptically, "What makes you think he'll be so obliging?"

"I been ticking off how I'd do it. There's different ways, but I was him, I don't reckon I'd send men up there to shoot down at our camp." Jonathan pointed with his thumb. "See that canyon to the south? We drove in through there, so following our tracks, he'll come on this valley from that direction. He'll see the herd bedded down on the wide end, and our camp at the narrow end. Fires, and what look like sleeping men. Brother Danziger just can't help himself; he's bound to want to stampede them cattle this way. Way the valley bottlenecks down, they can't go anywhere but over the camp. We'd never know what hit us. Safe and sound, and he needn't lose a man. *Sabé?*"

"Good thinking, son." Gideon waggled his white head. "Blame good."

Alex said quietly, "That's how you'd do it, Buck?"

Jonathan gave him a look of thoughtful irony. "Uh-huh. Baring my conscience, boy. That's you. You're my conscience."

"One you don't often listen to."

Jonathan chuckled. "But sometimes. Makes it worth it, huh?"

Alex said with a faint acridness, "I'd have to think about that," and folded his arms on his knees, rocking slowly on his heels. "I think it's too neat. A man could almost smell a trap, the way you have it set up."

Jonathan grinned, his eyes half-lidded with a cruel wisdom. "All he's a-going to see is a herd and a sleeping camp spread out for him. He's going to see how he can run that herd over the camp, and then he's going to come hellfire."

"Why?"

"Because it's that way, him or me. Got to be." Jonathan picked a burning twig out of the fire. "There ain't no bleeding hearts going to understand. No God damn pacifist like you. With you, everything's in the head. You ain't going to savvy how two men can look at each other and hate clear through, so hard it don't leave their guts till one is dead. That's the way with Brother Danziger and me. We both knew it from the start. Why, the Pig can't keep his hate from leaking out; even his men talk about it, or how'd Chino's cousin know?" Jonathan carefully pinched out the flaming twig between a calloused thumb and finger. "So what he'll do is what I'd do to him. He'll spot us and he'll ride straight in. If he was one step ahead of me, knowing what I know, shoe'd be on the other foot. But he ain't ahead; he ain't even nose and nose. No reason not to ride in, he'll think. It'll be"—Jonathan sighed and dropped the twig—"just like shooting fish in a barrel. Just like."

When twilight was fading the dun rocks to dust-gray, Jonathan put his plan into motion. The fires were built up; the men arranged their gear and blankets about the fires in a manner that from a small distance gave the impression of men soundly sleeping, dead tired from a long day. All of them were, too, but Jonathan's orders roughened them all to cool alertness; everybody had a part in tonight's work, and he wanted no mistakes.

A few men were to remain by the fires; he wanted

them kept stoked to a high, steady flame so Danziger
would have no doubts of a sleeping, unaware camp
when he first saw it. The rest of the crew was pulled
back from the valley onto the circling ridges, all of them
armed with cartridge-firing rifles. Each man dug himself into good shelter with a view of the open valley
below; their positions were sprinkled loosely on the
slopes, but Jonathan placed a tight concentration of
men around the mouth of the canyon where he judged
Danziger would come through. Once the thieves were
aware of being hopelessly trapped, escape would be
their first thought. Nobody, Jonathan stated, was to
escape.

Alex stayed by one of the fires, now and then feeding
it with pieces of mesquite. He didn't want to think
about what would occur, but he could not stop it. Here
at least he would have no part of the shooting; all he
had to worry about was getting out of the way fast if the
herd actually flared into motion and thundered onto the
camp. It could happen, even if Jonathan didn't permit
Danziger's people to get a push started; the trail-
skittish cattle could be set off by the first shots.

Among the men stationed by the canyon were
Jonathan, old Gideon, and even Paul. Alex wryly
reflected how Paul, even more than himself, disliked
violence; but Paul lacked his stubborn individualism
and self-determination. Paul was still a Trask, with a
duty to meet in his own eyes and those of his family if
living were to be halfway tolerable. Different as his
nature was, his ways were dependent, so he yielded to
the demands of family pride.

The boys, Cort and Liam, were with the second herd
two days behind them. Jonathan had overridden Cort's
hot insistence on accompanying the first herd, which
was the more likely to run into trouble. Alex supposed
that his warning to Jonathan about Cort's wildness had

taken to a degree. Jonathan was like that; he sometimes heeded Alex' advice where he would nobody else's. In small ways he'd lately curtailed Cort's activities with an eye to blunting his wild side and instilling an appreciation of hard, sober work. Yet Cort was still wearing his gun; his cocky manner had not been dented, and Alex had the feeling that at best such minor restraints were only a goad to his impatience. The only thing that would cure Cort with a fair certainty was a sound horsewhipping. . . .

Even the knife-edge of tension couldn't overcome a dead weariness, and Alex dozed time to time, elbows braced on his knees; but repeatedly jerked awake enough to keep the fire bright and high. Toward midnight he drew more alert, the restlessness of animals in herds at this hour being a notorious fact. It would be a likely time to launch an attack. . . .

The faint-drifting roar of a voice, Jonathan's, came from the heights upvalley. That meant, all of a sudden, that the raiders were in the trap, that the signal had been given. Then the crackle of rifle fire, echoes slamming between the rocky walls; whoops and cries of men in pain and battle lust carried across the herd, which began to make ponderous, ominous stirrings in the night. A wash of starlight frosted the soaring cliffs and gave a solid definition to the milling heads and horns of hundreds of cattle; otherwise there was little to be seen.

Hurriedly, along with the other men tending fires, Alex came to his feet with an armload of brush, heaving it on the flames. Hopefully the increased firelight, along with the handful of nighthawks, would hold back the restless cattle. A heavy ripple of motion coursed through the animals; panic was overcoming indecision, but so far their milling was aimless.

The steady pound of shots continued to shatter the

night, but already the battle was shredding into more occasional shooting. Over the other sounds, a man was screaming with a high, inhuman rhythm, as if wounded unmentionably. And a few horses were running—some Notchcutters breaking out of the trap or trying to. Alex had the obscure, startled thought of how millions of minutiae had to flow together for eons to converge in a climatic moment and how these crucial instances, for all their flurry and fury, were seconds in duration. Then they were history, the process reversed to an eternal diverging, affecting whatever they touched forever, like outcircling ripples. . . .

Jonathan Trask's fight with the Notchcutters was decided in less than five minutes, and with it the future of a vast piece of Texas.

The shooting ebbed off; Jonathan was booming and bellowing orders. From this Alex knew the remaining outlaws were throwing down their guns in surrender and the GT riders were closing in around the prisoners.

In a few minutes they had herded the handful of remaining outlaws into the firelight. Jonathan was hatless, his face like brown granite, and a bandanna was twisted around his bleeding left hand. His right hand still held his Navy Colt; he didn't train it anywhere in particular, but his fist continued to flex around the butt, relaxing and gripping, as if he could not let it go.

He sent a flinty glance across the men standing by the fires, then said tonelessly, "Build 'em higher."

They threw more brush on the flames; the orange flicker rolled across the GT men, the four prisoners, and Jonathan's big form, spraddle-legged by Alex' fire. To Alex' remark that he didn't see all the crew present, Jonathan said meagerly that the rest were on burial detail.

"Danziger?" Alex said.

Jonathan's beard jutted; he shook his head. "Him and his brother broke out. They got clear away. I think the two of them and one more man, couldn't be sure."

Slowly he moved over to stand before the biggest outlaw, a ragged, red-bearded man. "Where's Danziger?"

The man shrugged. "Don't know any Danzig—"

Jonathan backhanded him solidly before the last word was quite out; the big man took a step back, rubbing his mouth as it bled into his beard. "He was there," Jonathan said matter-of-factly. "Couldn't no more mistake a pig squealing. Tell me where you boys usually rendezvous at."

"I wouldn't kn—"

This time the smash of Jonathan's fist knocked the man to his knees. He stayed that way, shaking his head slowly. "We got all night," Jonathan said mildly. "I can last a sight longer than you. Figure on that, then figure how much it'll get you in the end."

"Iffen I talk up, I would count on goin' free."

Jonathan shook his head. "No. You're going to hang, the four of you. Only question is how hard you want to go. There's an easy way."

Jonathan tilted the Navy Colt a half-inch; he fired. One of the other three outlaws, kicked back by the bullet's impact in his chest, fell by a fire. His legs twitched; his outflung arm touched an ember and the sleeve began to smolder. A GT man took a couple of steps and toed the arm away from the fire.

Jonathan's words dropped like stones in the silence. "Your friend now, he got it easiest way I know of. Hanging like I do it is a sight harder way. Man's neck don't break and he cuts a mighty sorry figure dying. But there's a sight worse ways."

He lowered the pistol slightly, cocking it. "Here's one, Red. Elbows first. One at a time, no hurry. Then the knees, same way. Plenty other bones in a man's body to get busted. Never done it to a man yet, but I reckon he wouldn't cut half as sorry a figure dancing on a rope."

The red-bearded man did not argue at all. He told them were Danziger would probably go; he spat the words like venom. He gave the appearance, at least, of being more angry than scared, and his defiant fury did not relax as his hands were tied behind him and he was hoisted into a saddle. He cursed them with a steady, bitter monotony as he and his companions were herded on horseback over to a dead, gnarled tree at one end of the valley away from the fires.

The horses were quirted from under them; the three men kicked awhile in the reaching firelight. Jonathan watched as their lives were strangled away, and Alex forced himself to stand by and watch too. After a while he said, "That was damned raw, even for you."

"Three of ours was killed by the canyon. Pa was one."

Alex started; a coldness filled his belly. He'd assumed that both Gideon and Paul were with the burial detail. He turned his head slowly toward Jonathan, who continued to stare at the spastic dance of the three outlaws.

"Some ways I reckon Pa really died a long while back." Jonathan's eyes had squinted nearly shut. "Paul is back by the canyon with him. He went 'most crazy. Said he would shoot me if I even touched Pa's body. By Christ, I won't take no blame for that."

"For that—no," Alex said. "It was the shock, Buck. He had to take it out on somebody."

"A funny thing. We never got on, but I never knew till tonight that he purely hates me."

Alex said nothing for a full minute, then: "I don't

have to ask if you mean to go after the Danzigers—say at first light?"

Jonathan nodded, echoing, "First light," as he spun on his heel now, walking toward the nearest fire. Alex fell in beside him, pointing out, "Probably he won't go to his favorite rendezvous, even if he hopes some of his men got away and would join him there. He'd figure somebody you captured might give him away."

"I allow that, but a man gets habits. I allow he'll still head for his general bailiwick. And I mean to keep on his tail, him and them other two and any more I get wind of till there ain't a Notchcutter left in them parts. Not a live one."

"Suppose he runs fast and far and doesn't stop?"

"Then I'll hunt the Pig clear into hell."

This was the single token of Jonathan's grief anybody would see. From that alone, a man couldn't doubt that his father would be revenged to the hilt.

9

JONATHAN ORDERED THE MEN HE'D HUNG CUT down and buried beside the others. He had ordered the mass grave to be made deep and filled up with rocks and left unmarked. The GT dead, including his father, would be returned to the ranch and interred there. The cook's roustabout was assigned the task of conveying the three bodies in a *carreta* to Katytown and the undertaking parlor there.

Jonathan broke off the drive to Baxter Springs; he would leave a minimum of crewmen to return the herd to the GT pens while the rest of the crew followed him on a search for Alvah Danziger.

Before leaving, Alex tramped over to the canyon where Danziger's gang had been caught in the ambush. Paul was by himself under the starlight, sitting on his haunches by a silent, blanket-covered form. As Alex bent over it, Paul said softly, "Don't touch him."

"Paul—you can't blame Buck."

"Pa never thought I was the man I should be, and likely he was right. But I didn't mind so much, for it was the same with Cort and Li. Buck was the only boy of his he could see. I loved him even so, Alex. . . ."

"So did Buck."

"God damn Buck," Paul said in an intense whisper. "He's put the Indian sign on this family. Land and cattle, more land and more cattle—what's it all gone for? Pa is dead. Cort is growing up wild. And Mercy—it makes me sick inside to see how miserable she is. She still loves him. We could of been happy if he'd never come back. Get away, Alex. Now he's got you standing up for him. Get away from me."

More talk would be useless, Alex saw, and he went back to the fire. He now knew for a certainty that Paul could have no inkling of Jonathan's carrying-on with Mercy. Otherwise, hating Jonathan as intensely as he did, Paul's reaction would not be this vitriolic and remain passive.

As a gray glow relieved the night, Jonathan ordered the men to saddle. In minutes they were riding south. The red-bearded outlaw had told them of a cave in a caprock ridge a good ten miles north of the Trask ranch. It had been a favored place of Danziger's, though he was too canny to lay low very long in any one spot.

The night dwindled into full dawn. The sun was high when Jonathan, Alex, and the crew came to the ridge the big outlaw had indicated. Here they beat about through a heavy matting of brush till they located the cave opening. The entrance was so low a man had to duck through, but it was spacious inside. Here, by matchlight, they saw stores of food, cartridges, and other supplies.

"He aint' been here," Jonathan said. "But we'll make sure nobody has the use of this stuff. Lug it outside."

"Wait, wait," Chino Lucero cautioned. "Nobody walk around." He had picked up a lantern and lighted it, and now he paced a slow circle of the cave, holding the light close to the floor. "Haaah. He has been here. Him and the two others. Is plenty track in soft sand. The thin man, the Pig's brother, he is hurt. He limps. He is in a bad way, I'm think. The Pig was holding him up. Here he rested a spell while the Pig and the other man, they pack up some grub. Then they all go out. I ain't tell no more; all your big feet, they have tromped out the sign."

"Get outside." Jonathan's words were honed with tension. "Look around. See if you can't pick up the trail."

By beating through the brush, the GT men had erased any sign to be found near the cave's mouth; but after a few minutes Chino found a patch of mesquite where the outlaws had tethered their horses. Here was track enough to show that Lat Danziger, almost unconscious from blood loss, had been hoisted into his saddle by Alvah and the other man. Then the three of them had struck eastward toward a rim of stony hills that ended the sedgegrass prairies.

"They mean to lay up there," Jonathan said with a note of savage exultance. "All they can do now unless the Pig wants to leave his hurt brother behind, and I got a feeling he won't." He raised his voice. "You men get to lugging out that stuff in the cave. I seen some tins of coal oil in there. Douse it with that, all but the ammunition. Divvy that up. The rest I want burned in a pile. It'll be a marker to keep any and all thieves 'minded this ain't their kind of country."

While the men hauled foodstuffs and other goods from the cave, sorting out only the boxes of shells, Chino followed up the tracks the three outlaws had left, Jonathan and Alex moving behind him. Chino rode slowly, bent from his saddle to study the ground.

"They go pret' slow," Chino grunted. "The thin gringo, he drop plent' blood. They have to stop soon, I'm think, or he ain't last."

"How far ahead?" Jonathan asked.

"Two, maybe three, hour."

They rode on. Looking back, Alex saw the pyre of

Danziger's supplies erupt into billowing smoke; seconds later the men caught up with them. The sun climbed higher and they sweated and groused, chafing with impatience.

At the edge of the hills, the sign left by the three horsemen began to thin away on rocky, treacherous ground. From the way Danziger had often switched camps, it was a fair guess that by now he knew the country well enough to possibly elude his hunters a long while yet.

Jonathan, shredding a cigar between his teeth, said in disgust, "Christ. We should of packed along some of that grub."

Chino swung a long arm. "Just across them hills is where my cousin live, the one who help us. You like beans and coffee?"

"Not the way a peppergut likes it. Forget it. Keep on the trail."

"It goes that way."

They crossed the low range of hills, and a wide valley dipped away below. There were patches of good grass down there, and a herd of sheep was being hazed along by two men, one of them on horseback, the other afoot. "Ho," Chino murmured, and put his gaunt nag down the slope. They reached the bottom and approached the flock. The man on foot, a thin Mexican, raised his staff and said, "Good morning, cousin."

"Good morning, Sandal," Chino said. "What a pity you are not a *vaquero* and I must always look down on you from a horse when we meet."

Jonathan snapped, "He talk American?"

"Haaah," Chino said. "Sure, but not good like Chino, I'm think."

"Then leave off the spick so we can make you out." Jonathan was staring hard at the man on horseback, who had reined in a few yards away. He had apparently been idly trailing the Mexican, giving him little if any help with the flock, and that seemed curious. He was dark and narrow with a wind-chapped face, and there was a nervousness about him.

Jonathan said, "What's your name, mister?"

"Jess Mandel."

"Mostly we don't ask a stranger his business, but this is a different case. Better tell what you're doing about here."

"Been riding the line for my grub," Mandel said. "I stopped over at this Mex's place last night. Am helping him with his woolies to pay for my food and keep."

Jonathan clapped his stare on the Mexican. "That so?"

"Is so," Sandal nodded, beaming. He had a clown's face that was even uglier than his cousin Chino's. "Plenty so, fella."

Suddenly Chino murmured something in Spanish, the words so low and brisk and fluid that Alex, who understood the tongue well, could hardly follow. What Chino asked his cousin was whether the gringo was what he claimed to be.

He was not, Sandal replied with the same liquid swiftness. There were two others in his house, one of them wounded. They were . . .

Mandel understood something of their talk, or else he sensed the gist of the exchange. His hand stabbed to the percussion Colt thrust slantwise through his belt, but he had barely yanked it free when Chino's bullet smashed his shoulder. Grunting, he tried to bring the weapon level, and Chino's next shot drove him out of the saddle, dead before he struck the ground.

Scowling, Jonathan said, "What the hell? What did that greaseball say?"

"The Danzigers are in his house," Alex said, and spoke in fluent Spanish to Sandal, who nodded and replied at some length. Alex translated during the pauses. Sandal said that three had come to his house very early this morning, one of them half-dead from a bullet wound. They were on the run and had come to Sandal Rojas because they did not yet realize it was he who'd betrayed them. His place was isolated, and it was known that his wife, who was part Choctaw, had skill with medicinal herbs. She had treated the wounded one, Lat Danziger; but his fat brother, who gave the orders, was suspicious and careful. When Sandal had asked to drive his sheep across the valley to graze as usual, Alvah Danziger had sent this one, Mandel, along to watch him.

"The Danzigers are in his place?" Jonathan did not keep the heated exulting from his voice.

"They'll have heard those shots," Alex observed.

"Don't matter. The Pig won't leave his brother. Where's the place, Mex?"

Chino jerked a thumb eastward across the valley, and Jonathan kicked in his spurs and headed away. Sandal shrilled something, and Alex wheeled back. "What did he say?"

"Eh, his wife," Chino grunted. "Don't be afraid, little cousin; I will not let her be hurt." He heeled his mount after Jonathan, and Alex and the crew fell in behind. As they neared a motte of scrub oak, Chino cautioned them to go slow; the trees ahead hid the house of his cousin. To take the quarry by surprise, they should dismount and go through the trees on foot. At the edge of the timber, Jonathan halted and dismounted; he motioned them to do the same.

"Buck," Alex said quietly, stepping to the ground. "Rojas' wife is in there. Go easy now."

"Not for any squaw I don't." Jonathan said it between his teeth, his eyes like black stones.

Chino Lucero dropped out of his saddle like a great

cat, light on his feet, and his posture was ominous. Alex said swiftly, "Buck, don't make any mistake here. Do anything to endanger the woman, and you'll have more than a couple Danzigers to worry about."

Jonathan looked at Chino, then scanned the brown-black faces of his crew. All of them stared back, waiting, and Jonathan was no fool. His teeth flashed in his beard. "That's how it's to be, then. But don't make a mistake of your own, which would be you got thinking I give a damn what anyone thinks. I don't."

"Why," Alex said dryly, "that's a mistake nobody could make."

The men glided into the trees, Chino leading the way, slipping from trunk to trunk. The morning was still; percolations of sunlight flecked the brush-clean floor of the motte. Then they came into view of the house, and Chino sliced the air with his palm to call a halt. It was a small but well-built cabin of green logs nestled low in the sheltering timber along a creek bank. Off behind it a rambling fence enclosed the sheepfold; there was a small corral with several horses inside.

Dropping to his haunches beside Jonathan, Alex murmured, "We can probably make a deal for the woman's safey, if—"

"No deal," Jonathan interposed flatly.

"Wait. Haaah." The whispery chuckle escaped Chino as the door of the house opened a stealthy crack. A moment later the stock form of the half-Choctaw glided out, moving noiselessly for all her ungainly bulk. She was making her escape, Alex realized, just as Alvah Danziger shouted from inside, "Woman— you!"

She began to run across the brief clearing, and then Danziger's massive form filled the doorway; he was swinging a rifle to bear. Without a moment to lose,

Chino palmed up his pistol in a lightning movement and sprang out of the brush to meet the woman. He shot hastily, spoiling Danziger's aim, and with an astonishing quickness the huge outlaw leaped back into the cabin. Chino pulled the halfbreed woman to the shelter of the brush.

Jonathan, swearing luridly, pumped a shot into the puncheon door. Then the flap of oiled paper that half-covered the window was torn away; a rifle barrel nosed across the sill. Danziger fired, the bullet clipped off a leafy twig that dropped on the brim of Alex' hat. Jonathan grated, "Now. Pour it in," and opened fire again.

A salvo of rifle and pistol shots ripped into the cabin. Alex held his Colt in hand, but did not shoot; he coughed against the reek of burned powder, squinting at the cabin. He heard a brittle crash of crockery. The gunfire would be playing havoc with the Rojas' meager belongings. "For God's sake, Buck," he heard his own voice; and then Jonathan's order: the shooting slackened off.

Jonathan roared, "Danziger—come out, you fat bastard! I want to show you where my pa took a bullet in him!"

There was no answer. The cabin had a gutted, empty look, the door hanging wide open, one thong hinge shot in half so it hung crazily askew.

Alex heard a crackle of flames and a faint, gurgling scream. Smoke began to gush from the door and window. Not waiting, he left the trees and crossed the clearing at a run.

Stepping into the cabin's single room, Alex was half-blinded by the pouring smoke. He heard the scream again and saw a man thrashing weakly on a narrow bed at the end of the room, the bedclothes afire.

Alex plunged toward the bed; he stumbled over something and nearly fell. Catching balance, he took a recoiling step back. Alvah's monolithic body, the lower jaw blown nearly away, lay on its back, the eyes wide and sightless.

Alex stepped across the body and reached the bed, whipping off his coat to beat at the flames. Realizing the futility of trying to smother the fire, he tore at the burning blankets tangled around the wounded man. He ripped them away barehanded and rolled Lat Danziger off the smoking mattress to the floor. His clothes were starting to burn, but Alex smothered the smoldering patches with his coat. He tried to lift the writhing, shrieking man, but Lat's struggles made it impossible. Catching him under the arms, Alex, choking and half-blinded, dragged him across the floor.

Mercifully then, Chino and a couple of men were beside him; hands relieved his burden and other hands were guiding him out the door.

For a time after sinking to the ground outside, he could only cough and hold a bandanna to his watering eyes. Finally he could see again. The crewmen were running buckets of water up from the creek and into the shack. Sandal Rojas had arrived and was speaking to his wife in a low fury. Evidently she had left a lamp burning, the flame turned low, at the head of the bed. A shot had shattered the lamp, sending a spray of burning oil across the prone body of Lat. That did not concern Sandal, but it might have burned down their house, he pointed out furiously. As it was, the GT crew had gotten to the fire before it could spread; there was plenty of smoke, but little damage.

Jonathan ordered three men to carry Alvah Danziger's vast corpse from the cabin. Lat Danziger lay groaning on the ground where the men had left him. Despite a great weariness and the pain of his blistered hands, Alex got to his feet and went over and knelt beside Lat. His skin and clothes were so caked with soot and dirt and dried blood that Alex couldn't tell where he'd been wounded or how badly he was hurt. His face was swollen with livid weals, the hair and eyebrows singed completely away, and he was in considerable pain.

Alex started toward Sandal and his wife, intending to ask if there were any lard or grease available to coat Danziger's burns as well as his own hands. Just then he heard Jonathan harshly ordering someone to bring a rope. Alex pivoted in mid-stride, walking over to Jonathan.

"Did I heard you right? That's for Lat Danziger?"

Jonathan nodded, a wicked light in his black eyes. "Told you what would happen to these bastards when I caught 'em."

"But Buck, my God, the man's nearly dead now, wounded and burned—"

"That's just fine. He won't need but a nudge. Trouble is, it's most like doing the son of a bitch a favor."

Feeling a sickness that went beyond disgust now, Alex said, "Then don't. God, Buck—I didn't save a man's life for this."

"Then why did you?"

"A good dozen years ago," Alex said, making his voice calm, "I saved your life and got a leg ruined for it. Does that count as a debt in your scheme of things?"

Jonathan ran a hand through his thick beard, the heavy lines of his face settling in a wry squint. "It does. Get it out."

"All right. I claim a life from you, Lat Danziger's life. If he spends the rest of it in prison, even your tender sensibilities should be satisfied."

"Done. But you mind that squares us."

Alex said edgily, "You can put it in writing for all I give a damn," and walked away from him.

10

THE POWER OF ORGANIZED OUTLAWRY IN THE region was broken with the demise of the Notchcutters. Lat Danziger's long and painful recovery terminated in a life sentence in the penitentiary. There were still the usual trifling brush-runners and ne'er-do-wells around to scavenge off honest men's hard work, but they were in the category of everyday and unavoidable nuisances, like nits and taxes.

There was still plenty for Jonathan to do outfitting his ambitions, and he set his teeth directly into the job. He had said accurately that the future of Texas depended on two things, the vast increase in longhorn cattle and the demands of a hungry public in the East. The northern ranches had a crying need for beef stock too, a mature high-grade animal fetching up to fifty dollars on the current market. But the obstacles between the Texas cowman and that market were brutal and discouraging. The northbound drovers who swung east ran into the fever quarantine and the plowed fields of angry farmers, while the warlike Comanches made a westward swing just as perilous.

Following his father's funeral, Jonathan again set out for Kansas with his two herds. He got them both through to Baxter Springs, but lost a total third of his cattle to Indians and Jayhawker stampedes. Two of his men were killed fighting off the raiders.

He sold them at a skimpy profit to a Yankee buyer, got drunk for a week of nights, and was preparing to start back for Texas when he met a Midwestern entrepreneur named Joseph McCoy who talked of rosy times just over the next rim.

McCoy, it seemed, had friends among the officials of the Kansas Pacific railroad which was building west, eventually to Denver. There was a good chance he could perssuade them to build shipping pens and a siding at a Kansas station by stressing the big payroll spending in any trail town and the freighting boom of transporting cattle to Chicago. McCoy had his eye on a Butterfield stage stop at Mud Creek about a hundred fifty miles southwest of Kansas City. The Texans would have a ready and reasonably handy railhead market for their herds. No farmers, no quarantine, only a warm welcome, a fair shake, and cash on delivery. He wanted to promise the railroad that no less than a million cattle would be shipped out the first season. He was asking every cattleman to spread the word far and wide through his own district, up and down the trail, of a sure market and a square deal.

Through the year that followed, Jonathan bought all the cattle he could in anticipation of a tremendous market boom. Meantime he turned his hand to other financial concerns—and even civic duty.

Though organized outlawry was wiped out in the region, the maverickers who had been rounding up and trailing unmarked stock north since the war were making appreciable inroads into the unbranded cattle still running wild on ranch-owned range. Jonathan, like every ambitious cowman, had done his own share of mavericking; but he was instrumental in having the driving of stock from its native range punishable by a fine and jail sentence unless the drover could prove ownership. Because enforcing the "Act of '66" was almost impossible on the vastness of the Texas plains, Jonathan urged his neighbors to roadbrand all their trail head, a practice he had followed since the war.

His reputation widened as a champion of progressive methods; but the innovations he prompted meant more gold in the Trask pocket. He built picket pens by Chisholm's trade road south of Belton and charged fifteen cents a head to roadmark northbound herds, often slapping a common brand on large herds which already bore the brands of a half-dozen ranches. Biding his time, Jonathan made no trail drive during the fall of 1866, but he turned in a solid profit branding thousands of head for other drovers.

By next spring, he felt less confident; most Texans had cause for jitters. There was a depression in the East; the newspapers reported long queues of unemployed being fed at the Tombs in New York City, and the food was not beef nor even beef broth. The demand for beef was greater than ever, but there was little money available to buy it. By midsummer, with McCoy's new town of Abilene a reality, the sunken market had many cattlemen bitterly declaring their decision to make no drive this year.

Jonathan, always ready for a calculated risk, threw two large herds on the trail. He was hoping that if enough cattlemen stayed home, the tight, limited market that did exist would offer bonanza to the drovers who arrived first. He could command his own price.

It was a shrewd gamble, but it fell through. A cholera epidemic that began among the soldiers guarding the Kansas Pacific tracklayers had spread through the state like wildfire, even to the drovers on the trail. Half of Jonathan's own crew came down sick, and three of them died. He was stalled on the trail for several weeks, and when he finally reached Abilene it was to learn that the first trainloads of longhorns had already reached Chicago and the depressed East; prices had plummeted.

Jonathan wrote it off as the kind of bad break a man could never take account of, setting his sights on the year to come. And the 1868 season, to be sure, got off with a bang. The Chisholm Trail was overhung with a blanket of dust on all its now-meandering branches, and Abilene was chockful of waiting buyers. Cattle poured in by the thousands, destined for the stockyards and feedlots in Illinois, for the stocking of ranches as far north as Montana, for the quotas of agency beef the government had promised the northern tribes. Abilene itself was, of course, roaring and wide-open; drovers' wages flowed into the town coffers like water; whiskey and blood flowed the way they always did.

It went that way throughout June, which saw a thousand cars full of cattle rolling toward Chicago. Then, early in July, a new Texas fever scare swept Kansas and other states where Texas beef had touched. Out of the seventy-five thousand cattle that reached Abilene that year, a full three-fourths found no buyers, and as with the year before, the all-over season proved out unprofitable.

That was no concern of Jonathan Trask's; he had been among the early arrivals, and he returned to Texas with a gold-laden pack horse, surrounded by his well-armed crew. Along the way he told a number of northbound drovers the bad news about the tick-and-fever scare dropping the bottom out of the Abilene market. Most of them simply changed their destination, but a few, fed up by one too many years of miserable returns, sold out their herds to Jonathan for next to nothing, and he hired enough men from their crews to drive the cattle home.

Promptly on his return, flushed with success and

more exuberant than anyone had seen him in years, Jonathan threw the biggest and best celebration the country had ever seen.

Though it was still summer and the weather mild, sleeping tents were set up for the guests. An area was cleared for dancing and a platform raised for a five-piece band. All the calf wagons were put to use hauling supplies from town, including cases of bourbon and rye; mostly staples, for the women from the surrounding ranches would provide the delicacies such as cakes and pies and jellies dear to the palates of working hands and sorely missed on the trail. Preacher Boggs was invited to officiate at a camp meeting for those who wished to attend one. With all arrangements made, riders were sent out in all directions to welcome the ranchers, their families and crews. The women of the Trask ranch kept busy scrubbing clothes and children; the men scraping away or trimmed their beards and washed themselves raw in the creek, and shined their boots with lampblack.

Mercy and Samantha were busy till the last minute making ready. The old house had long been a head-quarters for Jonathan's far-flung and constantly enlarging range of activities, and the increasing weight of her duties as hostess and house-keeper was wearing Mercy to a wan shadow. Temperamentally and physically, her tolerations for daily stresses were sharply limited; more and more she was leaning on the sturdy and indefatigable Samantha.

Being childless, the former slave lavished all the love and loyalty of her fierce, protective nature on her mistress. Mercy gratefully accepted this reversal of roles, for her gentle, dependent nature could hardly bear up under what it was carrying already.

Though Mercy's clandestine affair with Jonathan had been going on a good three years, Alex was fairly certain that nobody outside of Samantha and himself was aware of it. Samantha could always be depended on to see everything and to say nothing. Even he was sure of what was going on only because his accidental knowledge of one meeting of theirs had kept him uneasily alert to small signs in their behavior that indicated nothing had changed between them.

Otherwise he wouldn't have paid particular notice to Mercy going off on what seemed like a casual stroll by herself. Not long after, Jonathan, who was helping Alex dig some barbecue pits not far from the house, sauntered off in the same direction. He needed to stretch his legs, he said.

Surprisingly, he returned inside of ten minutes, and went back to work without a word. He looked faintly stunned, even bewildered. Something had hit him hard; he might be boisterous or harsh depending on his mood, but he was never retiring; it was his nature to roar his feelings. Yet through the rest of today he spoke only when necessary, and his face continued to hold a bemused, faraway look that was not angry, not happy, just the look of a man not sure what he should feel.

11

THE GUESTS BEGAN TRICKLING IN EARLY NEXT morning. The Trask brothers and Alex personally welcomed each new arrival and assigned each rancher and his family to a tent. Beef ribs bubbling in grass-fat suet in a barbecue pit sent a delicious aroma across the camp that honed every appetite, lifted every spirit and set the mood for the three days of feasting and dancing that would follow.

Samantha, heading up a retinue of Negro woman, wives and daughters of the crew, took efficient charge of all the culinary activities. She also had the task of seeing that all the colored people—a good many freemen having settled in the Yegua district since war's end—were made welcome in their own part of the camp. No tents were provided for them, but there was straw for pallets and an abundance of food and drink.

The first night was a gala one, with eating and drinking, talking and laughing; two squares of dancers swung before the campfires; the men talked over mutual problems of range and trail, and the women chatted endlessly. The Reverend Mr. Boggs moved from group to group, exchanging pleasantries with the ladies, having a single glass with the men and a warning stare for the heavy quaffers: his mere glance showered brimstone.

Alex, alerted by Jonathan's behavior of yesterday,

had had a watchful eye on both him and Mercy
throughout today's proceedings. Jonathan was drinking
heavily, something he was rarely known to do. Mercy
had a nervous and abstracted air; and finally Alex saw
her break off talk with some women and walk over to
Preacher Boggs.

The circuit rider had paused in his gregarious rounds
and, gently nodding in time to the music, was watching
the dancers. He glanced at Mercy as she said something; he gave a genial nod, and the two of them walked
off a short distance. Again Mercy spoke and even a
good thirty yards away, the flickering firelight showed
the agitation in her face. Quite unexpectedly, Preacher
Boggs wheeled, lifting his long arms; his millennial
voice boomed for silence.

"Brethren, now leave off your merrymaking and
listen a spell. Listen!" Mercy plucked desperately at his
sleeve, her lips plainly forming, "No—no," and her
expression at that moment was one of clear, agonized
fright. Boggs was not looking at her; beaming at the
gathering, he boomed, "She's retiring and modest as
becomes a woman, is Sister Trask; but this is a proud
time in a woman's life. And a man's. Brother Paul
Trask—where is he?"

Someone shouted for Paul; Mercy seemed to quickly
recover, or rather gain a resigned composure, but Alex
understood that the preacher had mistaken what she'd
meant to impart. A *confession?*

Paul, smiling but bewildered, came over from a
barbecue pit, men slapping him on the back and passing
joval quips. The Reverend Mr. Boggs threw one arm
around his shoulder and the other around Mercy's, his
long face shining with a happy benevolence as he told
the assemblage what everybody was already onto, that
Sister Trask was with first child.

Paul gave his wife a swift and searching look. Then

he was shaking hands to right and left, smiling and nodding to a score of well-wishers. But a troubled shadow lurked behind his face, as if he were putting together a hundred minor, once-unrelated observations.

In Alex' mind there was no doubt at all, not even before he noticed Jonathan heading away by himself toward the dark grove along the creek bank. His steps were unsteady; he detoured enough to scoop up a double-eared jug of corn from a table loaded with homemade potations. He tilted the jug and pulled deeply, and moved on into the night, jug swinging from his fist.

Alex' concern at the moment was for Mercy. Sickly and overwrought as she was, she was probably close to a breaking point after what had just happened. He waited till the crowd pressing about her and Paul began to break up, then edged over toward them.

Paul, still nodding absently to the congratulations, detached himself from the group and started away, his brow clouded by uncertainty that a casual onlooker would take for mere preoccupation. He passed Alex at three yards' distance without even a glance at him. Feeling a small alarm, Alex halted and followed Paul's progress across the camp. But he did not seem to have anything particular in mind; he simply walked away toward the house till the darkness swallowed him.

A couple of minutes later, Alex was able to catch Mercy alone. She had gotten off by herself behind a deserted wagon. She was standing there looking across the prairie, a worn *reboza* hugged tight round her thin shoulders though the night was warm.

"Mercy."

She came swiftly around, her eyes dilating in the starlight. He said, "You all right?"

"You know . . . Alex?" Her whisper turned almost

inaudible as he nodded. "I thought you did," she murmured. "You're always trying to help us, all us poor weak fools. Nobody can help us any more."

"Couldn't be mistaken, could you?"

"No. Samantha knows about these things. She said—"

"Wasn't my meaning."

"Oh . . . no, there's no mistake. Don't you think I'd know if there was? Even Paul—poor Paul—has finally guessed the truth. Did you see his face?"

"I saw it."

"But he can't be sure. Dear God, he can't be. He hasn't a way of knowing how far gone I am. Not yet, but when the baby is born so long after—"

"Mercy," Alex broke in. "It's time you braced up. No more of what's been. The baby can make all the difference—"

"I'm weak." The words wailed softly from her. "You can't know how weak I am!"

"I know. That's why the baby can make all the difference in the world. It can be like the strength you never had."

"Every time I look at its face—every time, Alex!"

"No," he said flatly. "It won't be that way unless you let it be. Mercy—if you could do for your baby what you never could for yourself alone, it could mean a new life. For you, for Paul. Make him believe the child is his—you can make him believe it because he loves you, because he'll want to believe. God knows it's a white enough lie." He paused grimly. "As for Buck, he'll leave you alone from now on."

"Oh, you know how he is!"

"Maybe I know better than you. Will you ask me to be the baby's godfather?" She looked at him in bewilderment, and he said, "As godfather, I'll have a stick to wave at Buck. I'll tell him in so many words he's to stay the hell away from you, and if he doesn't, if he ever does anything that might hurt my godson, I'll load up a shotgun with scrap iron and empty it in his belly."

She continued to stare at him, incredulously now, and he said wryly, "That doesn't sound like me, I know. But Buck knows me better than you—a sight better than anyone. He'll know it's no bluff. He knows I'd never say it unless I meant it."

Alex left her with that thought; she needed time to assess her feelings. Meantime Jonathan needed to be told a few things; if he weren't too far gone in drink to listen, there was no time like the present. Alex headed for the woods, in him a quiet surprise of his own hard-handed interference. He was reluctant to meddle, but there was no other way to head off disaster. After he'd talked to Jonathan, he might do well to hunt up Paul and josh him a bit and urge him to have a drink or two. It might somewhat allay his suspicions till Mercy could speak to him.

Through the trees ahead, the stars gave a sparkling sheen to the black creek water. He could hear Jonathan, guttural with drink, tunelessly bawling a song. The trees ended by a steep cutbank, and Jonathan sprawled against it on his back, knees pulled up, heels dug in the wet gravel at the water's edge. Alex dropped down beside him.

"Listen, Buck."

"Call me Paw, you sonuvabitch. Gonna be a paw soon." Jonathan hooked a finger in the jughandle and swigged deeply. Then in a haze of drunken fury, he swung the jug at Alex' head. Alex moved nimbly aside, the jug thudding on the turf. With a vast, alcoholic sigh then, Jonathan rolled quietly on top of the jug, clasping it to his belly, and dropped his bearded head against the bank. Alex took a handful of his hair and lifted his head and then, seeing he was out cold, let his head settle back, turning it enough to keep the sand from shutting off his air. He was tempted, though.

Alex stood and brushed the sand from his trousers, gazing speculatively down on the sodden man. All he could do was let him sleep it off and try again later. He started to ascend the bank, but had taken only a step when there was a harsh crackle of brush as someone broke free of the woods.

It was Paul. He stood on the bank above them, his eyes wild in the murky whiteness of his face. He held a heavy Army Colt in his hand; it was lifting from his side, and Alex felt a thickness of fear clot in his throat.

"That's what I thought," Paul whispered. "That's why I went after the gun, so I could put the question to him and make him answer. I heard him just now. So I don't have to ask. . . ."

The time for words, any sort of bluff, was past; Alex did not waste a word even to divert him. Now he would be lucky to prevent murder. Having no gun, Alex threw himself up the bank as Paul started to cock the pistol. He dived and grappled Paul around the legs, and felt Paul smash downward viciously at his head. The blow missed, the gun barrel slamming across his shoulder. With a savage heave, he lifted Paul clear of the ground and threw him.

They tussled back and forth, fighting for the gun. Alex was the smaller, his trim-muscled body the lighter, despite Paul's gauntness of frame. Paul's physical condition was never much to brag on, but he had enough Trask size to use his weight where it counted, smothering Alex with his trunk and pinning him. They were teetering on the edge of the cutbank; Alex heaved sideways with all his strength, rolling them off the brink. They hit the water on their sides with a shallow splash, but Paul fell in deeper water; his face went under; he coughed and strangled. Alex wrenched the gun away from him. He jammed the muzzle against Paul's ribs, hissing, "Quit it—quit it now!"

In his rage Paul paid no heed; he reared wildly up, upsetting Alex, and for a moment they thrashed around in the muck. Then the pistol made a muffled bellow against Paul's body. He jerked as if broken in two; his mouth came open and the light died coldly in his eyes. Still holding onto Alex, he slumped slowly against him and the strength ebbed from his grip.

In horror Alex shoved him away and watched him roll limp as a rag in the dirty shallows, his head lolling.

"God—Paul?"

Jonathan groaned and mumbled something. He was still dead to the world, and Alex gave him a moment's blank regard. Then he floundered to his feet, bent and caught Paul under the arms and dragged him up the bank. He straightened, feeling a chill bite through his wet clothes; the enormity of what had happened hit him fully. He hadn't meant to pull the trigger; he hadn't even realized that sometime in the struggle the gun had gotten tripped to full cock.

There was a savage, stunning irony here; he'd tried to stop Paul more for Paul's sake than to protect Jonathan. But well-intentioned action or not, Paul was just as dead.

He was not sure how long he sat that way, wet and cold on the bank beside a dead man and a drunken one, before the sound of someone's approach through the brush roused him.

Chino Lucero stepped onto the bank; his black glance stabbed and weighed the scene in one restless glance. He dropped on his haunches beside Paul's body. "He try for kill the big Trask, I'm think," Chino said very softly. "Haaah. Chino watches things and sees much. But I'm think the big Trask was too drunk to do som'thing like this."

"I did it," Alex said hollowly. He made the explanation brief.

"I'm hear the shot," Chino said then. "Nobody else pay much attention; I hear only the one shot, maybe fired in play, I'm think. But I been watching things and I'm not so sure. So I come look."

With a wrenching effort, Alex shook away the numb shock gripping him; he met Chino's stare across the body. "Can't let the truth of what happened here get out. Do you follow me?"

"Maybe I know, but maybe you better say it plain, hah?"

"If what really happened and what led to it gets out, a lot worse will follow. For Miss Mercy. For her unborn child. You know what the word scandal means?"

"Haaah."

"I'm not concerned for myself, Chino—the shot was fired accidentally, and we'll tell it that way. But a little differently. We were clowning, the three of us here, me, Paul, Jonathan, passing the jug back and forth. The horseplay got out of hand. I was fooling with the gun—it went off by chance. That's how it happened. You agree?"

And Chino nodded, his eyes blank as smooth china in his coffee-dark face.

12

PAUL TRASK'S DEATH PUT A SUDDEN PERIOD TO the celebration. He was buried two days later in the walnut grove beside the graves of his father and mother. A dismal rain fell during the brief service. The weather matched Alex' mood, but both would pass in their time, he knew. He was no Trask; he might be enmeshed in their problems, but he was master of his passions as no Trask could ever be. And he could live with what had happened.

As for Jonathan, he'd been too far gone in liquor to be even dimly aware of the truth. Alex was tempted to throw that truth in his teeth, but knew he never would. It would do no good; nothing would ever humble Jonathan, not even guilt, and he must be bearing as much as he could feel. The brother he'd cuckolded for three years was dead, and for days Jonathan was ugly and unapproachable with the weight of his thoughts.

Then, Alex allowed, there was the welfare of Mercy and her baby to be considered. With the woman he'd always wanted free at last to wed him, there seemed a good chance Jonathan would pull out of his doldrums, soften his nature, and do his best to become a good husband and father.

Within the month Preacher Boggs said the words that made them man and wife, but even before this, Jonathan's surly anger at life evaporated as if it had never been. He bent every effort toward building a new kind of life for himself and his family-to-be. He bubbled with plans for his unborn son (always for a son). He hovered around Mercy with the outsize presence of a mother bear, seeing that she didn't exert herself, that her least wish was not neglected. One had the feeling he was engaged in a constant effort to suppress a shout of sheer exuberance in living.

Yet the new state of affairs had a tainted undercurrent. When Jonathan was with her, Mercy showed a quiet happiness, full of her love for him and letting him see nothing else. But several times, catching her alone, Alex saw her staring into the distance, her whole manner vacant and withdrawn.

He supposed she had reasoned out a fair approximation of the truth, that Paul had been killed in an attempt on Jonathan's life and that she and Jonathan shared blame for his death. Perhaps the strength of her love for Jonathan let her hold the ghosts of shame and guilt at bay, if she couldn't wholly exorcise them.

Thought of her approaching motherhood also furnished Mercy with a happy distraction. She spent her days sewing on infant garments and letting Samantha handle the ordeals of hostess and housekeeper. She ate well and got plenty of sleep to build up her strength.

Everything seemed to be going well until she went into labor weeks ahead of time. All that day she fought waves of excruciating agony while Jonathan paced the parlor muttering over and over, "If she dies . . . if she dies . . ."

Alex was with him when Samantha, her magnificent stamina frayed by hours of vigil, came into the parlor at last. "We lost the baby," she said in a flat, faraway voice. "Mrs. Trask, she well, but she's weak, her. Now she's sleeping."

Jonathan stood tall and heavy-shouldered in the

center of the room. Alex was struck anew by the unconscious power the man exerted, his presence dominating the moment with an intensity that overwhelmed. Without a word then, he turned on his heel and tramped from the house. Minutes later he was riding away from the ranch. Watching from a window, Alex saw his quirt flailing up and down.

First of all, when Mercy awoke, she called for Jonathan. He had not returned, and she began to sob weakly, hurt to the quick by his desertion. Strong and soothing, Samantha's words had a calming if not reassuring effect on the girl; she slept again.

Jonathan did not come home that night, or the next, or the night after that; and then word drifted in that he had been involved in various drunken brawls at one roadhouse after another. Alex realized then how large a part Jonathan's plans for the child had played in briefly remaking his character. Jonathan Trask was an empire-builder; like all such men, he saw his ambitions in terms of dynasty.

When he returned a couple of weeks later, he did not seem greatly changed at first. He was even chastened and apologetic, and Mercy quickly forgave him. Still both of them had been changed in ways barely perceptible; as time went along, the variables became sharper, more apparent.

Jonathan had never been more than an occasional drinker. After a doctor told him that any future pregnancy would put Mercy's life in jeopardy, he took to drinking a good deal, not enough to impair his efficiency, but enough to keep insupportable thoughts in their place. A good many men, some of them great men, did as much all their lives, Alex knew; semi-alcoholism was something a man could live with, but the shame of it was that something had gone out of him forever, a part of courage.

Physically, Mercy's recovery was complete; but more and more frequently she slipped into those spells of mental absence. Sometimes, busy at a household task, her fingers would grow idle; her eyes would turn vacant and she would begin to speak in a soft, toneless way, at times to herself or to the dead Paul, but usually to nobody in particular. She might be alone or with others, it made no difference. If, to snap her out of it, somebody gently spoke to her, she would jerk guiltily back to the present.

Gradually she became fixed in two worlds, separate and distinct: one the sane, normal world of any ranch wife where she functioned perfectly, alert if not happy; the other a dim limbo of her own into which, unbidden, she might cross at any time.

After a few months she got no worse and no better either. And that was how matters remained with Mercy Trask.

Jonathan, meantime, reverted back to the callus of an ambition which dictated that no amount of success was ever success enough. In this regard, at least, all things went his way.

It was another boom year in 1869 for McCoy's Abilene; the number of cattle shipped had doubled, one hundred and fifty thousand head going out in two thousand cars.

The following year the number doubled again, and three hundred thousand were conveyed out by the railroads, which were now engaged in a bitter rating war. These were growing times; and riding with the tide, Jonathan tripled his fortune. To carry home his yearly bonanza in Yankee gold coin (in accordance with the general Texan distrust of paper money since Confederate currency had turned worthless) he had a special chuckwagon built to his specifications; it contained a false floor with a hidden compartment beneath. Some of his money stayed in Kansas, invested in a variety of mushrooming enterprises.

Despite rumors of growing unemployment in the East, everybody predicted that 1871 would be the greatest year the cattle industry had known. But Jonathan, too many irons in the fire claiming his attention, got a late start north this year. Not long after his departure, word came down the trail that Abilene had been shut down. Alex, left in charge of the ranch as usual, wondered if Jonathan's luck had run out at last.

But Jonathan returned as always, in a flush of elation. As soon as he'd gotten wind of the rumors, he had left his herd and hurried on alone to Abilene. He'd met Shanghai Pierce just leaving, and got the story from that angry old wolf of a cattleman. Abilene's own delirious boom, of loose money and easy sin, had choked off its young life. Antagonism between the Texans and the Abileners had mounted to fever pitch, and the city fathers had worsened matters by hiring Wild Bill Hickok as marshal. The town had become a cynosure for tough and cocky gunmen from all over. When brash young Wes Hardin took the redoubtable Wild Bill's guns away from him, it was a red flag to all the tough ones. Wild Bill downed Phil Coe in a gunfight, then accidentally killed one of his own deputies. The upshot of the matter was the town council declaring a hasty termination of Hickok's job, and Wild Bill just as hastily departing Abilene for reasons of health. The Texans simmered down then, but proceeded to depart in droves, feeling the town had given them the raw end of things.

It was clear that Abilene was finished, and old Shanghai said he was sending word to his own herds down the trail to swing southwest to Ellsworth. That had also seemed the best alternative to Jonathan, and he'd turned his own herds along the same route. But buyers were scarce in Ellsworth; Shang Pierce decided to hold his cattle there until he could dicker a deal with somebody, and he managed to peddle a few head to the government.

Jonathan was more fortunate; making the rounds of Ellsworth's saloons, he fell into talk with the Yankee representative of a British firm who was looking over prospects for his company. He'd already bought some prime acreage near Fort Kearny, and intended throwing mixed stock on it. Inside of an hour Jonathan had him out sizing up one of his own three herds; he'd made a deal on the spot for all three for a gross profit of one hundred and fifty thousand dollars.

All this was well enough, but Alex had news of his own and it wasn't good. Every sign pointed to a new wave of rustling in the area, the first since Jonathan had cut the ground from under Alvah Danziger's Notch-cutters five years ago. But this operation was of a different nature, so scattered and small-scale that it probably wasn't organized.

The quickness of Jonathan's fuming wrath at this news surprised Alex; he said: "Nothing to throw a fit about. I thought you should know, is all. If a man owns the whole dog, he doesn't rile over a few nits who stake their claim."

"That don't make a God damn bit of difference. Nits make lice. Let a few of 'em start up and get away with it and you got a hundred to deal with before you know it. What the hell've you done about it?"

Alex shrugged. "Not a lot. Put out trackers and had Lou Mapin look around. Most we can tell in a general way is the trouble is coming from the Bittercold Creek bunch. What can you do? Some are guilty, some aren't, but blood's thicker than water and the honest ones will cover up for the others. Try taking direct against anyone on his home ground among friends. Even with irrefutable evidence—and we have none—I wouldn't care to take on a whole countryside."

Jonathan chewed his dead cigar and paced the office floor. "What's behind it all? Them Missouri rawhiders been settled around the Bittercold country a good three years now, and we had no trouble till now."

"I have an idea why," Alex said dryly, "but I don't know there's any making a big, successful man like you understand it."

Jonathan halted, eying him with annoyance. "What's that?"

"Well—eking out a bare living isn't enough. A poor man may steal, even when his need isn't quite pressing, out of a pure desperation and defiance. By preference, the man he'll steal from is the man who has a hundred times his own needs. In these parts, that's you. It's the price you pay for being big."

"The hell it is!" Jonathan spat out the cigar butt.

Alex sighed. "Well, I told you."

"That I wouldn't get it, huh? It's clear as glass, counselor. A pack of lazy, do-nothing jackals who can't stand seeing a better man top 'em because he shows 'em the guts and spirit they ain't got."

"That pretty well sums it up. But I don't see what you can do except ignore it."

"I'll show you what." Jonathan stabbed a blunt finger at him like a knife. "That old bastard Cady is the one. Speaks for the others, don't he? Somebody got this business started, and it had to be him. They follow his lead."

"You're wrong," Alex said patiently. "That old man is as honest as they come."

"You know him all that well, eh?"

"By sight only. Beyond that by reputation, and his is

a sound one. Everybody who's had dealings with Cady says as much. If his whole bunch isn't all wool and a yard wide, why blame him?"

Rufus Cady, from what Alex had heard, had held a battlefield commission in the Grand Army of the Republic. Before that he had been a supporter of the late John Brown. His position and vitriolic frankness had made him less than beloved among the native Texans since he'd moved from Missouri with his sprawling clan to see if he could raise the family fortunes in the ranching business. All the ranchers north of the Bittercold Creek had two things in common: all were Missourians related by blood in one way or another, and all looked to Rufus Cady for leadership. In spite of Cady's ruffling many feathers, everybody grudgingly conceded his integrity to be dead center.

"We'll see," Jonathan said grimly.

"Cinch up," Alex said. "I told you there's no evidence against anybody. You can't pass sentence without proof—not even you, with due acknowledgment to some of what you've gotten away with. Not and stay out of prison."

Jonathan said dourly, "You ever get tired of being my conscience?"

"Yes," Alex said flatly.

Jonathan's disproportionate anger at the petty thievery did not slack off as time went by; he was careful not to go too far, but he took steps. If he had suspicions about a particular Bittercold neighbor, he would hazard a guess as to his own loss, and that neighbor was likely to find that an equal number of head wearing his brand had been mysteriously shot. Alex knew that Jonathan was giving several of his crew, hand-picked by Chino Lucero, secret orders through Chino as to what should be done where against whom.

By the end of the year, Jonathan's increasing toughness against the continuing depredations had churned up an undercurrent of public resentment. It did not build quickly, because plenty of people who resented Cady's outspoken federalism were willing to believe the worst of him and his people, but Jonathan's harsh retributions were alienating many more, especially after his mathematical slaughtering took in stock of several ranchers not allied with the Bittercold crowd. Even his friends were finding a reason for fearing him.

Jonathan reacted to the public criticism and resentment with even harsher moves. Alex protested in vain: the loss of a few cows could not be worth a fraction of this snowballing antagonism. He was talking against the wind; in Jonathan's eyes the least act against his interests was a challenge flung in his teeth. It was a question of time as things got worse before they became intolerable—then something would have to break.

13

WHEN THE 1871 CATTLE SEASON SWUNG around, Jonathan's cattle had weathered well one of the bitterest winters in Texas memories; he threw his biggest herds yet on the trail for Ellsworth, full of expectations.

Cortney, now twenty-two, and Liam, turning twenty, stayed behind at the GT for the first time in years, despite Cort's hot objections. As usual Alex was left in charge of the headquarters, and Jonathan took him aside before leaving.

"Watch Cort," he said tersely. "Hear me?"

Alex eyed him skeptically before saying. "You know, I've had the feeling something happened on last year's drive. What was it?"

Jonathan glowered and hedged, but finally came out with the story. One night in camp Cort had quarreled with a new man; they had pulled their guns together, and Cort had killed the other. To all appearances it had been an even play and Cort had been the faster, that was all. But the incident had set badly with the crew; to a man they felt that Cort had crowded the other to a fight, and one or two voiced the opinion he'd done so deliberately. Jonathan didn't give a damn what they thought, but a reaction had showed in their surly obedience and fumbling work, and tongue-lashing them till his throat blistered hadn't helped. Probably the feeling would carry over if Cort accompanied this year's drive, so he was staying home.

"What you're not quite saying," Alex said dryly, "is there could be a repetition of last year's trouble."

Reaching his seniority had only worsened Cort's wild and vicious streak; little about him reminded Alex of the bright-natured youth he'd been. Ironically, the pliancy that had once made Cort almost too agreeable, too willing, had proven the weakness which had led him to take a harsh-natured older brother as his idol, his example.

"What the hell," Jonathan did not quite shout, "do you mean by that?"

"You know what I mean. I told you years ago when I said, take the gun away from him." Alex paused, then added flatly, "I won't be responsible for that kid, Buck. I can't control him—nobody but you can. Most of the time, at least. And I won't be responsible for what happens if you leave him here. He hasn't been far from you at any one time in years. If you want to take the chance, I can't stop you, but it's on your head. He needs looking after more than Liam."

Jonathan glowered some more and cursed, and then said he'd leave Chino behind to look after Cort. Chino Lucero was the man with enough presence to exert command over even Cort, Alex had to admit, but whether Chino was a wise choice in any other respect was debatable. Chino had an unbridled streak of his own which had been tamed only minimally from answering to Jonathan for so long. But Alex couldn't think of a better solution, and it was settled that way.

After Jonathan's departure, Alex kept the three of them busy with a full roster of assignments—Chino, Cort, and Liam, who could handle most range jobs well enough if he weren't left alone. Chino accepted any work cheerfully; Cort groused a good deal and called Alex a slaver, but Alex thought grimly, *Idle hands and the devil*, and kept them hopping.

Since the house had been enlarged, Alex had a whole wing to himself: a bedroom, a study, a room for storage. He liked the time when the ranch was almost deserted for the annual drives: the ranch books were up to date and there wasn't much work to handle. He gave the skeleton crew their assignments each morning and had most of the day to himself. Best of all, the house was quiet. Only the two women were about, and Mercy was as subdued as a mouse; Samantha went about her household duties like a shadow.

One morning some weeks after Jonathan had left for Ellsworth, Alex was looking forward to the day with a special pleasure. A new Zola novel and Thoreau's *Cape Cod*, two books he had sent for months ago, had arrived late yesterday. After he'd issued the day's orders, he intended to retire to his study for a few hours' good reading—till the day's first problem came up. One usually did before long, but maybe he'd be lucky.

As always he took breakfast with Mercy and the two Trask boys; Samantha served them. Cort dawdled over his food and Liam followed his example. Alex finished eating, pushed back his chair, and with a peremptory word to both to get a move on, left the house and headed for the corral where the crew was assembled to receive the day's orders.

Halfway across the yard he saw a horseman coming through the east pasture gate, and in a few moments identified him as Lou Mapin. The sheriff was not coming from the direction of town, and at this early hour that seemed curious. Some business or other must have taken him out in the pre-dawn hours.

Alex halted and waited, and Mapin put his horse directly over to him. "Morning, Lou. Light down."

Mapin said, "Morning, Alex," making no move to dismount. "Don't reckon Buck's back from Kansas yet."

Alex said no, he was in charge, watching Mapin's expression with mounting alertness. The years hadn't touched Mapin to speak of; he was still ambling, just competent, and given to a mild favoritism toward the Trasks. That was why Alex noticed at once the set weather lines around his eyes and the tightness of his jaw; his whole manner was unlike Mapin.

"Better get it out direct, Lou."

"Well, there ain't no other way." Mapin leaned forward, crossing his arms on his pommel. "A couple Bittercold men are dead, and it was pure murder. It looks like something that was ordered done, and the look points this way. Mind I ain't saying I believe it, Alex."

"That's good," Alex said hollowly. "Killed how, Lou?"

"Happened up by Redemption Creek, northeast o' here. A couple of them Bittercold boys, Tris Drucker and Morton Gant—they both are shirttail relatives of old Rufe Cady and work for him—was found just this side of your line, or close to it." Mapin hesitated. "The sign round the place looks like they'd made off with a few GT steers and somebody caught them skinning out the carcasses."

"I asked you how."

Mapin pursed up his lips and turned his big right hand over, regarding the palm blankly. "Well, these GT cows they taken was skinned out like I say. Drucker and Gant was trussed up and wrapped in a couple of the hides. I make it happened early yesterday sometime, and the sun was at 'em all day. You know green rawhide when she gets drying."

"God," Alex whispered in disbelief. "You don't mean they were put inside—alive—"

"They was alive, and I reckon for a good while. Takes a spell to die that way. You see the looks on their faces they died with, you'da believed it."

Alex lowered his chin and scrubbed a hand slowly across his face, then looked up again. "I'd like to know who brought you the word."

"Rufus Cady's boy, Struther. Cady was worried last night when Drucker and Gant didn't report in. Thought they might of gone for a whoop in town, but when they wasn't in by first light this morning, he and his son went out for a look. They knew where Gant and Drucker had been ordered to work out yesterday, so they went along the Redemption and found 'em directly. Then the old man sent his boy in to fetch me. Went to see for myself before comin' here."

"Look, Lou—" Alex paused, trying to frame what he wanted to say. "You won't say you believe we did it. All right, what do you believe?"

"Don't know what to, yet. It was all tramped up around the place, no sign a man could make out. I want to ask was any of your men working out that way yesterday morning."

"Cort was," Alex said slowly. "Li was with him. Chino Lucero, too."

"They always work together, the three of them?"

"Lately, yes. Since Buck—" Alex broke off; the explanation would worsen the implication. "Since Buck left," he finished lamely.

"Alex, you hear me now. I looked the other way for plenty from the Trasks. They been my friends since Gid rode me on his knee when I was a tad. I recall how you and me and the Trask boys would cut up sometimes on the cow hunts and old Gid would roar. Me and Buck and Paul, we-all enlisted in the Matheson County Volunteers same time. Anyhow I allus figured there was plenty justice on Buck's side when he went after the Notchcutters with his own sort of law—there wasn't no other kind could of done the job. And I know this Bittercold bunch has been putting on him with penny-ante thieving." Mapin stopped abruptly, shaking his head. "But Jesus, Alex. No decent man can look away from this."

"Nobody's asking you to, Lou. And nobody knows better than me how hard Buck can crowd. But he's always made a point of never concealing his actions, and he's always seen to any job of that nature personally. He didn't order this done, and neither did I."

"Well, somebody took it on themselves. I want to talk to Cort and Li, Lucero too."

"Right away." Alex glanced toward the corrals where the crewmen were waiting their assignments. He told Mapin to wait a minute or two, then went over to the men. He gave them their orders casually, making no mention of the trouble. He told Chino Lucero to come with him and went back to where Mapin waited as Cort and Liam came sauntering out of the house.

Mapin repeated for the Mexican and the two Trasks what he'd told Alex, and Cort's response was prompt and hot. He threw down his cigarette and heeled it into the earth. "If I'm accused of killing a couple men, I want to hear it said out!"

Alex watched Cort's face carefully; he could detect nothing but honest outrage and his usual temper. With his full growth Cort was only a hair shorter than his brothers. He closely resembled the late Paul at the same age; trim and lean and wiry, almost slender, with intense, nervous features that reflected every feeling. That far, the similarity was striking; from there on you noticed only the differences.

"Nobody's saying it," Mapin murmured. "Just want to hear what-all you boys done yesterday and where you went."

Chino and Cort gave easy, consistent replies to Mapin's queries. Liam couldn't get out much that made sense, but that was to be expected. Liam had grown into a young hulk, somber and heavy-browed. His eyes were intelligent, though the rest of his face was not, and its dullness was deceptive. Nature had left something out of Liam, call it a social vitality, but he was not stupid. Though he could rarely express himself coherently except by writing his thoughts out, his understanding was clear as a bell. He was almost inseparable from Cort, but he knew the difference between right and wrong; he could never had faked the shocked, bewildered effect Mapin's words were having on him.

Finally, impatient with Mapin's line of questioning, Alex put in, "I'd like to ask something, Cort. Was Li with you the whole time yesterday?"

Cort gave him a bland, easy glance. "Not every minute, no. Is that important? We all split up now and again and fanned out. We was turning out the brush along the creek for calves, and it went faster if we broke up."

"You didn't keep in sight or call of each other all the time?"

"Not all," Cort said in a mildly ruffled tone. "Alex, don't tell me I got to swear to you I'm innocent?"

Alex said flatly, "You'd do better to worry what a grand jury'll believe," then swung around on his heel, hands rammed in his pockets. He scowled at the ground, absently listening to Mapin drone more questions. Cort's facile, unworried air, his touch of injured irritation, left Alex unsure. He told himself, *You don't know anything yet, so go slow.*

He swung around again as Mapin grimly said, "I want y'all to ride out to the Redemption with me. I want you to see this business with your own eyes. You too, Alex, so you'll have no doubts. After, if any of you is hiding something, any old thing that might help find the killer, he'll maybe change his mind."

They rode northeast across the rolling sedgegrass. The wind undulated the grass in gentle waves; the morning was quiet except for the stir of horses, the creak of leather.

Alex gave Chino a thoughtful, lid-narrowed glance—the Mexican's dark, ugly face was sober, maybe a shade bored, exactly as you would expect an innocent Chino to react to a possible murder charge. His carefree manner was sloughed, and that was all. Alex was less sure of Chino than he was of Liam, yet he couldn't believe that Chino had taken part in the grisly killing. His streak of Spanish devilry might make him capable of it, but Cort's good behavior had been entrusted to him, and the more he thought about it, the more he believed Chino would take that trust seriously. He couldn't blame Chino for not feeling he'd had to watch Cort every minute, yet suppose Chino had reason to suspect Cort of covering up something— would he speak up? For in the muddy uncertainty of the situation, one thing stood out starkly: Cort was the only person at GT whom he'd unequivocally believe capable of unprovoked, cold-blooded killing.

The Redemption was a muddy straggle whose banks were matted and overgrown. As they rode, Chino and Cort pointed out the different places they'd split up to divide the work, guessing at how long they had been apart each time. On at least two different occasions early yesterday, they'd been apart an hour or more. *Long enough,* Alex thought.

Mapin said at last, "There's the place." He pointed at a liveoak motte set back from the creek, and swung his horse that way. A wagon and team were pulled up by the trees, and two men were standing by it. "Old Man Cady and his boy," Mapin explained. "They brought the wagon out to take the bodies home. I told'em to leave 'em be till I could fetch you out."

Alex glanced at him. "This could be trouble, Lou."

"I reckon not. I made it clear to Cady I won't stand for any. No need to tell you too."

"No." Alex shot a warning look at Cort, who faintly smiled and shrugged his shoulders.

Alex had seen Rufus Cady only once or twice, never without the Spencer repeater he always carried, usually on his saddle but never leaving it in his boot when he left his horse. It was not a killer's weapon; what it seemed to grimly declare was that Cady wanted trouble with no man, and the rifle was to prevent trouble. He was a medium-tall man in his late fifties, pared down to bone and lean muscle. He wore plainest linsey clothes; his beard was a frosty bristle, his face brown as old oak leaves after frost and deeply troughed by time and weather. He stood with the rifle in the crook of his arm, hipshot, and looked over each of them as they rode up. He said, "One of them?"

Mapin said, "You give your word," as he stepped to the ground.

"It'll be kept. We'll wait long enough to see what kind of justice we get from you, Mapin."

"That could be up to a judge." Mapin moved forward into the grove, Alex, Chino and the two Trasks following.

The wrapped corpses in their hide covering lay in the

tall grass. The hides had been slashed open, probably by young Cady when he'd found them. The bodies inside were enough exposed to leave no doubt how they died. They had been bound hand and foot with pieces of rawhide *riata,* doubtless their own; the hides had been wrapped tightly around them and stakes driven through the hides to anchor them fast to the earth. They were far enough from any tree so that the sun, broiling down all day, had gradually and excruciatingly drawn the green hides hard and tight till their iron embrace had tightened off wind and circulation. The brands on the hides had been turned plainly up: each was a GT.

Alex forced himself to look for a full half-minute, then he turned away, the muscles in his throat knotted. "Death of the Skins."

Mapin looked at him sharply. "What?"

"Death of the Skins. I've heard of it. A Spanish trick."

"Ever been used hereabouts?" Cady demanded. Mapin shook his head, and Cady's hawklike gaze pounced on Chino Lucero. But he said only, "You find out anything from these rich people, Mapin?"

The sheriff told him what little he had learned. Rufus Cady listened in silence while Struther Cady, fingering one of the new repeating Winchesters, moved up beside him. He was about twenty-five, a black-haired young man inches taller than his father; he was rawboned and lean as a hound's tooth. He had dark eyes that were quick and feral. As Mapin finished, he said swiftly, "That's enough to arrest the three of 'em on."

"Like hell he will," Cort murmured.

"Shut up, Cort!" The flat coldness of Alex' voice rang startling in his own ears, but its sharpness cut through the moment's tension. "Lou, you have Judge

Sharpe set a date for a hearing. We'll come in then. I want this thing cleared up."

Mapin stroked his chin and said in a moderate voice, "Reckon that's how it should be."

Alex swung a glance at Cady. "These boys have any family?"

Rufus gave him a long stare, as if debating whether to answer. Finally he said, "Mort was an orphan. Tris, he had an old pap and mam he was sending all he made. The boys was both kin, and I had 'em in my care. That's a trust."

Alex nodded, then dug a roll of bills from his pocket. "Money can't pay for a life, but Drucker's father and mother will need this. Two hundred and fifty dollars, all I have. You can send them two hundred; the rest will pay for a funeral."

Struther Cady said hotly, "Don't take it, Pa! He's trying to buy us off their backs."

"Watch your mouth, boy," Mapin put in flatly. "I don't know how much of what's his Alex McKenna has give away over the years to folks in need, but it's plenty. Everybody in these parts knows the kind of man he is."

"I heard." Cady nodded. "McKenna, you and me ain't met formal, but you're one man I never heard any but a good word said of."

"I can say the same."

"You heard me cussed for a God damn nigger-lover, ain't you?"

Alex smiled faintly. "Could be if we're different there, it's because you roar."

"Maybe you whisper, but I got an idee you make yourself heard all right." Cady tipped his rifle downward as he hooked both thumbs in his jeans. "We can bury our own, McKenna. But Tris's folks can use the money, that fifty too. I'll put in some of my own and see they get it all."

Alex handed him the money, and again Struther began a furious objection, but his father cut him off sharply: "I ain't taking a cent for us, just for this dead boy's old folks. And I'm taking it from this man where I wouldn't from any damn Trask because I know by God when a man means it. You dry up all that jaw, boy, and go fetch the wagon here." Rufus bent with his knife to cut the dried hides and ropes from the two bodies, and Struther tramped sullenly away to the wagon.

As they started back toward the GT, Alex felt Mapin's thoughtful glance. "Alex," he said, "you ought to talk up more often. Could of gone bad back there, Cort and the Cady boy kicking up their spurs, if you hadn't put Cort down fast."

Chino was amused—"Haaah"—but Cort was not, and he reined angrily over to Mapin's stirrup. "He didn't put nobody down!"

Mapin only eyed him a trifle wearily, and Cort flushed and said defensively, "Well, Buck left orders I got to do what Alex says, but that don't mean nothing. If Buck was here, you would of seen things really handled."

"Yeah," Mapin said dryly. "Nobody needs to second-guess how Buck would of handled things. Only thing I can't be sure of is how many men would of come away from this slung across their saddles."

14

MOST OF THE TEXAS DROVERS WHO HAD FOL-
lowed Shanghai Pierce to Ellsworth after Abilene's
demise in '71 hadn't been as fortunate as Jonathan
Trask in finding an immediate buyer. More than forty
thousand cattle wintered in the region next winter, so
that when the 1872 season came in full swing, Ellsworth
succeeded Abilene as the leading shipping point on the
Kansas Pacific. It was another prosperous year for
everyone concerned, the only disgruntled note coming
from the wintering drovers who had not only had to
bear a heavy expense for the use of holding grass, but
had to settle for less than top prices, their steers having
aged past prime.

Jonathan returned to the Yegua country in the late
summer after the usual successful drive and sale of his
herd; he was becoming phlegmatic about success. He
was in excellent physical condition from hard work
straining the booze out of his system, and trigger-
tempered because he hadn't taken a drink in weeks.

Learning about the bizarre murder of Drucker and
Gant made his wrath flare like sparked gunpowder. He
raged around the office a minute or so, then wheeled to
confront Alex, who was patiently waiting for his anger
to taper off. "I suppose *you* think Cort done it?"

"I don't know," Alex admitted. "I know Liam
didn't, and I doubt Chino knows anything."

"Jesus. Only a God damn Injun would kill like that. Look, suppose'n them two had enemies among their own kin. If somebody taken out a grudge on 'em, a good way to throw off suspicion would be to wrap the bodies in a couple hides with the Trask brand."

"That's possible, of course." Alex' tone was skeptical. "Lou Mapin would have covered that angle in his investigation, I'm sure."

Jonathan snorted. "Wouldn't make no mind how many questions he ast, those people would stick together for each other."

"Not Rufe Cady," Alex said positively. "If he had sound reason to suppose any of his people guilty, he'd turn 'em over to Mapin, kin or not."

"Why you so almighty sure of Cady?"

"It's an impression you get of a man—not something you can explain. Look, Lou hasn't turned up a thing that says guilty about any party. The hearing next week will set out the known facts and show we have nothing to hide. The grand jury won't indict and it'll never go to trial."

Alex, Chino Lucero, and all the Trasks but Mercy, who hadn't been off the ranch in years, rode in for the hearing. These days Katytown was showing the flush of a mild prosperity. A steady flow of Yegua longhorns up the trail had brought back a steady flow of Yankee gold; people had money and they wanted to spend it.

Riding in this morning, Alex saw all the signs of new businesses on the way in; he felt the old twinge of guilt that hadn't troubled him in a long time. He took special note of the professional building that was going up along-side the courthouse, and the old daydream of a law office, a practice of his own, gripped him in a musing that held as they all dismounted at the livery and turned their horses over to the hostler.

Court wouldn't convene for a good hour, so the Trask brothers headed for a saloon while Alex sauntered around, still musing as he watched the carpenters at work. Finally he drifted into the general store and looked over the saddles, falling into a friendly hassle with Old Montrose, the proprietor, about the price of a secondhand one. "You damn' Scotchman, why don't you cut loose and buy a new one?" Montrose was saying good-naturedly, then looked past him with his old face pinching up into a bland stiffness that barely masked disapproval. "Do something for you, Miss Cady?"

Alex stood by a counter resting his palms on the saddle he had been eying. For a moment the name barely registered; then he turned his head quickly. The sharpness of his reaction brought the girl's head around too. It was surprise that had made Alex look; something else kept him looking; he was vaguely aware of this and he knew he shouldn't stare, and yet couldn't stop.

She was nineteen or a little more, and she wasn't pretty by any stretch of fancy. She was tall for a girl, not quite the height of an average man but able to face Alex eye-to-eye. Her figure was on the thin and wiry side, almost boyish but for the fullness of breasts which gave more than demure roundings to the loose drabness of the homespun dress she wore. The skirt was neatly patched in several places.

Her face was arresting in a way; he couldn't say how unless it was a composite effect, because every feature was distinctly wrong. Her mouth was too wide and full, her straight nose too long, her face too thin, angular as a boy's. Her eyes were a fine level gray under straight tawny brows, but her gaze was direct as a man's—very unbecoming, or was it only disconcerting? He disapproved anyway; she was too sun-browned and her hair, streaked almost white by the sun, was done in a careless blond braid that hung down her back nearly to her waist.

She met his stare indifferently, then looked away. She was a rawhider girl, and Old Montrose treated her with the cold politeness her place deserved. *Cady.* Alex frowned at the saddle, still wondering about the name, when Struther Cady came in. He glowered briefly at Alex, then moved over by the girl. Then Alex could be sure; she was as fair as Struther was dark, but their features were almost twinlike.

Old Montrose began filling the order, most of it bulky staples he had to drag from a storeroom at the rear. Struther hoisted a heavy keg to his shoulder and carried it outside to a big freight wagon. The girl bent to wrestle up a heavy sack of flour, and Alex said unthinkingly, "Here, let me help."

She gave him a very level look and said, "Thankye," and surrendered the sack. Alex grabbed two corners, lifted it with a practiced knee, ducked his shoulder to take the weight as his arms swung it back, and started for the door. He almost collided with Struther whose angry look shot to the girl, then back to Alex. "Give me that!" He took a rough hold on the sack and knocked off Alex' hat swinging it to his own shoulder. He said hotly then, "You keep a distance from my sister—any of our women, you hear me, McKenna?"

"McKenna," the girl said in surprise. "Is he—"

"He's a friend of them Trasks!"

"Struther, didn't Pa mention him? Pa said—"

"I don't give a damn what Pa said! Dammit, Jo, you been told and told to put down any stranger that talks to you!"

"By you, nobody else," she said heatedly. "If you figure I'm a little kid needs protecting, it follows I ain't old enough to be trusted with buying supplies. Do it yourself, sorehead—you can load it all up too." Her face was colored with anger as she marched to the door, pushed her brother aside, and went out past him.

"Ah, JoAnne—Jo!" Struther cursed as he tried to wheel through the door after her. He was overbalanced by the heavy sack which hit the doorjamb, burst open, and spashed flour across the floor. Struther stood swearing bitterly; he looked at Alex and swore again, then tramped out the door.

Alex bent and picked up his flour-spattered hat; he dusted it off carefully and set it on his head, then looked gravely at the speechless proprietor. "Don't guess you're in the mood for any more small talk, Monty," he observed, and left the store.

The courtroom was crowded, and the crowd flowed out around the veranda and windows of the courthouse. It was only a grand jury hearing whose outcome seemed foregone, but the grisly murders of Drucker and Gant had excited a good deal of attention. It meant a welcome break in the humdrum of a long summer, besides which just about everybody was convinced that the Trask boys and Lucero had done the job, and that Buck Trask had ordered it done before he'd left for Ellsworth. Despite the recent swing of public opinion against the Trasks, an approval of drastic measures against rustlers had put a surprising number of people in the Trask camp. A lot of them found no moral objection at all in an act which had disgusted even Jonathan—and that took some doing.

However, the testimony by Sheriff Mapin, by Cort and Chino Lucero and Alex himself, by Rufus Cady, became matter-of-factly dull with repetition. Liam, inarticulate with excitement, was excused from testifying. Only Struther Cady threatened to lend a heated note when he took the stand, but Judge Sharpe kept him sternly in hand.

Watching Cort's cocky blandness, Alex was strongly tempted to call him back to the stand and tear his story to pieces. A glib, tough cross-examiner could have shredded his facile defenses—assuming that he had anything to hide—and Alex was angry with the court for not providing a better one. He had to forcibly remind himself that he was present for the defense, that he wasn't only expected but obliged to stand solidly for his client's interests. Above all, he must not let his private dislike for Cort influence his objectivity. Sift it as fine as you pleased, there wasn't a ghost of tangible evidence except the thinly circumstantial against anyone.

No indictment was handed down; the court adjourned and the crowd outside broke up as the spectators began filing out. On impulse, Alex pushed his way to the side of Rufus Cady, who was moving toward the door with his son and daughter. When Cady turned to him, though, Alex found he didn't know what he wanted to say. He finally stated lamely that he wished Mapin had been able to learn more.

"So do we," Cady said, his eyes hawk-irised. "But I wonder why you feel called on to tell me so, McKenna. Ain't got a doubt about the men you defended, have you?"

"If he ain't," Struther snapped, "he damn well ought to—"

"Just shut your jaw," Rufus cut in with a tired note. "I want to go by the law, McKenna. I got an outspoke way that puts folks in mind of a fire-eater, but the fact is otherwise. Fire's no diet for making a life on. The war taught me that. Me and mine got a chance here, and I don't want to have to fight for it. But don't think because I made myself swallow this business, I can be pushed a lot further. Trask better not make that mistake. You tell him."

"I will," Alex said. "Anything you want me to tell him about the cattle he's been losing?"

Rufus lowered his head a half-inch. "I have got wind a few of my people was responsible, but I hate reading Scripture to any man. I talked soft to the ones I suspect, and it ain't helped. Now I'll bust them if need be and bust them hard. That's my promise."

He nodded briefly and moved on, Struther too, his face sullen. JoAnne Cady gave Alex that very direct, disturbing look, and he thought she might say something, but she followed her father and brother without a word.

Alex went to a saloon with Jonathan and the others for a victory drink, then went to the livery to claim his horse. This whole business had left a sour taste in his mouth, and liquor would not kill it. He was glad to leave the town behind and get onto the prairie under a clean hot sun. He went slowly on the road, presently coming over a rise to see a heavy wagon bogged in mud in the swale below. It was a marshy place badly filled when the road was graded, and after a thaw or a heavy rain it was always a treacherous crossing for a loaded wagon.

Alex rode down to the wagon and pulled up by a front wheel, touching his hat. JoAnne Cady was alone on the seat, talking quietly to the horses. Her handling of the team was strong and steady; she did not fight the reins or get angry, but the back wheel had sunk almost axle-deep into a pothole and she was mired solidly.

Again her level, appraising stare. "Reckon I'm hung up in here good. Don't want to take nobody out of their way, but reckon you could give a hand?"

In this country it went without saying that nobody in

trouble went unhelped, particularly a woman, but there was a stiffness in her tone. For a moment Alex thought this reflected a hostility over how things had gone in court, then realized quite suddenly it was only the backwoods shyness of a girl to whom strangers were almost unknown. Even her direct gaze that he'd thought almost bold was only ingenuous; yet she was uncomfortable and did not want to show it.

"Certainly," he said, and swung to the ground. "Have to lighten the load in the wagon bed somewhat, though."

"I'll he'p." She fixed the reins to the seat and stood, setting a foot on the wheel. Alex stepped over and put his hands up to her waist, bracing himself because she was all of his size; she set her hands on his arms and started gingerly to let him take her weight. In that instant, he started to swing her down, her foot slipped on the wheel—she simply dropped fully onto him. Alex' boots skidded and he went down flat on his back in the mud, JoAnne Cady on top of him. She made a muffled, mortified sound and fought in a half-panic to push away from him, her hands and knees getting no purchase on the slick mud. He groaned as her weight smacked squarely down on him again. With that, though, he had a brief wild awareness of the young, wiry life of her, the writhing warmth and squirm of quick thin muscles.

They got disentangled finally and floundered to their feet. Both of them were smeared with black muck from head to foot, and standing ankle-deep in mud, snapping it from his hands, Alex felt his temper come up—damn such a big clumsy horse of a girl. Then he saw the almost horrified mortification in her young face as she stared at his mud-plastered suit.

"Oh, I—I just can't say how sorry I am. My God—er, goodness. I sure didn't mean—"

"No harm done." He smiled with a great effort. "Let's get up on dry land and see what can be done about it."

They slogged out of the mud and tore up handfuls of dead grass to rub away the bulk of the mud. "What you grinning at?" she said with a hot and abrupt resentment.

"I was grinning *with* you, Miss Cady, if you'd been grinning, that is. It's kind of funny."

"It ain't funny at all!"

"All right," Alex said moderately. He supposed it wasn't at that, for her. Her wet, muddy dress was probably the best she owned.

They set to unloading the supplies stacked in the wagon, which took awhile because each heavy crate or keg had to be carried through the lake of mud that surrounded the wagon to dry ground.

"Leave the lighter stuff," Alex said. "See if you can ease it out now."

He held out his hand, and she eyed him a guarded moment before taking it, supporting herself as she stepped onto the wheel and up to the seat. Alex swung back on his horse as she gave the team a sharp hooraw. The horses leaned into the harness and the wagon stirred forward, but it was going deeper in the mud, the whole stern canting abruptly as the right wheel sank halfway to the hub.

"Whoa up," he said, and unslung his *riata*. Reining his mount around to the other side of the wagon, he shook out the coils and twirled out a huge loop, flicking it easily over the hub of the rear wheel on this side, the one less deeply mired, then over the wagon box. Alex spurred his horse away to take up the slack, then gave her a nod. JoAnne's shout sent the team surging into the harness, and Alex put his horse's straining weight into dragging the lariat taut. Slowly again the wagon budged and, as the sagging offside heaved suddenly up, the heavy vehicle rumbled free of the mud.

In a few minutes, working with a paucity of words, they had the wagon loaded again. Alex picked up his rope and coiled it as he walked to his horse. He felt the familiar heavy ache that always attacked his leg after it had taken a heavy exertion, and then he felt JoAnne Cady's stare. Ordinarily his limp was barely noticeable; now it was stiffly pronounced, and he felt a sudden fury of resentment against he wasn't sure what.

Again he stepped into his saddle, only then looking at her. He did not want to; he wanted only to say a quick goodbye and leave. She spoke first, saying swiftly, "That was right fine roping—way you handled the wagon too. I never seen better. You give me a start there."

Alex eyed her narrowly, his reins lifted. "Why?"

"Well, Pa said you're a lawyer fellow, and I could see today you're right at home in a court of law. And so fine-spoke and all." She smiled, and he could see her faint embarrassment. "Way you handle a horse and rope give me a start, that's all."

Alex settled his hands to his pommel, feeling about as sheepish as any damned fool. She had stared, then seeing he was offended, had quick-wittedly covered with a compliment that was not supposed to deceive him, only salve his abraised pride. "Well, I grew up with a horse and a rope and I'm still with them."

"I should of guessed that's how you took a bunged-up leg," she said seriously. "A body can't work horses and cows all his life without getting stove up now and again. Least-ways I never knew anybody did."

Alex was surprised by her quick, sure wisdom. Seeing he was mollified, she hadn't hesitated an instant in bringing the disquieting point back into the open where it belonged. He had to grin. "I guess that's right." He glanced back toward Katytown. "Where are your father and brother?"

"Pa has some all-day business to tend to. Struther says he is going to drink up a storm, so I left him to do it. There's only three of us now, Ma being two years gone, and somebody ought to be on the place." She swung up unaided to the high seat, quick and sure-muscled, and picked up the reins. She sat the high seat straight-backed, her hair a honeyed nimbus with the sun at her back, taking a man's eye without meaning to. "Hope they don't have a run-in with them people of yours, I supposed they stayed to get lickered up too. What you stand up for a man like that for, anyway?"

"I stood up for three of them."

"I mean the big Trask, one they call Buck. They say you're his best friend. Now I met you, it just don't make sense."

"Sometimes you don't choose friendship—either of you. It chooses you."

"Is *that* s'posed to make sense, now?"

"Maybe not," he smiled. "But if you have a friend, you take his side when he's right and try to turn him right if you figure he's wrong. I haven't turned him much, but I've slowed him down now and again."

"When has he been right? I'd admire to hear what you can say for a man like that, Mr. McKenna."

"A man like that," Alex said slowly. "A man too big to play it small. You didn't know him as he was once, Miss Cady. I did, and I saw what changed him. If he was to blame for letting himself be changed, then all men but a few saints should be blamed for being no less pliant when the chips are down. And God knows he's no saint. The thing is, his mistakes had to be giant-sized because his nature wouldn't let him do anything in a small way."

"But that ain't right," she said angrily. "It's like you're saying nothing he ever done was his fault."

"Faults? He has a wagonload. But the wrong he's done doesn't make the people he's dealt with right. He never set out that I know of to get anybody who hadn't wronged him. I hate war, Miss Cady; almost no war I've ever read of or heard of was justifiable by either side—yet a few were, because there's such a thing as one-sided aggression and you have to meet it or go under. That's the kind of war Jonathan Trask fought for this whole country a few years back, and because he did, it's a decent place for men to live and raise their families. I railed against his methods, but rattling an empty scabbard would have been just as wrong. And yes, the way he bulls ahead hurts the wrong people sometimes—but why not reserve a little of your indignation for the right ones, Miss Cady? I'm thinking of several of your good neighbors. Because whatever else Buck Trask may be, he's never been a thief."

JoAnne Cady said glacially, "I'll say good day to you now, Mr. McKenna."

Alex nodded with a chill dignity, saying, "I'll bid you the same, Miss Cady," and made an ironic gesture of touching his hat. A clod of drying mud caked on his sleeve crumbled away and thudded on his shoulder, which didn't lend much to the support of dignity.

15

WHEN HE GOT HOME, ALEX AVOIDED QUESTIONS by slipping unseen into his quarters and changing his clothes at once. The brothers returned quite late. Liam looked miserable, but not from drinking; he hated liquor. Jonathan was half-drunk and wearing a vicious stare that dared anyone to cross him. Cort was barely able to stand, and booze wasn't all to blame; his clothes were torn and dirty, and his face had been chopped to raw meat. It seemed he had run afoul of Struther Cady; a few hot words were exchanged and subsequently Struther had beaten him to a pulp. It was the fact of Cort's defeat, not his sorry condition, that had Jonathan upset. He shredded an entire cigar to rags between his teeth while he was talking about it.

Cort didn't appear for breakfast next morning. Jonathan's brooding anger held, and nobody had much to say. Halfway through the meal Chino Lucero entered the house unannounced, with the news that he'd found a piece of fence broken on the east side of the horse pasture this morning. He judged that six prime saddle horses had been driven off, and the sign said that a single night rider had done the job. Jonathan promptly reached for his hat, and Alex decided to ride along.

The three men struck eastward along the bank of the Yegua, Chino picking up the trail. Though the area was heavily brushed, the rider seemed to have driven his steal across the most open and sandy places; track was plentiful, and that seemed curious, as if he'd wanted to be quickly followed.

Within an hour they came on the horses on a sandbar projecting from the bank. But the sight of them was enough to make a strong man sick in his guts.

All the animals were alive, but each one had been brutally, senselessly mutilated in one way or another. Two had been hamstrung in both hind legs. Two of them had their tongues cut out. Two had their eyes gouged clear out of the sockets.

They must have been tied and thrown down and the dirty work done, Chino observed with the true Spanish indifference to cruelty. Jonathan simply stood and cursed, and it was clear that what angered him was having good saddle stock ruined. Alex could not say anything—he did not want to look at the pitiful sight, and he could not look away. The wanton shame of this was more than he could bear, and his eyes stung with gratitude when Jonathan, still swearing steadily, yanked his Winchester from its boot and, walking from horse to horse, ended the suffering of each.

Jonathan whispered, "God damn," staring down at the dead animals as the last rifle echoes died away in the morning. "What sort of an evil bastard would cut up fine horses like this?"

Hard on the heels of his words a heavy slug cut through the brush and slapped into the hindquarters of his mare; the animal screamed and half-crumpled, then went down. The three men broke into motion at once, lunging for the thin cover of brush along the bank.

They waited pressing against the earth, their guns out. Alex hadn't seen a thing, not a trace of powder-smoke or a stir of leaves. There was not the shadow of a sound. Close to the ground he could smell earth and green plants and the odor of waterside rot; the insects took up a broken humming again and the sun moved on the water—everything was normal.

After a while Chino eased onto his haunches and looked at Jonathan, who nodded, squinting at the wall of greenery. Chino faded into the thickets. Finally he whistled sharply, and the two of them rose and walked through the brush to where he was squatting.

"He was on foot and he is gone," Chino reported. "Eh, he's plenty good in brush, this fella. Ain't no Injun, I'm think, but he don't leave enough track to follow." He pointed at some shallow scuffs in the ground. "He is squat here and get a clear shot."

Jonathan growled, "That God damn Struther kid?"

"Haaah," Chino snorted. "I'm not think so. He is hot-head; he come straight on, he don't think something through. This fella here, he take plent' time and think her clear through, eh? Then he don' shoot at none of us, jus' the horse, an' he is gone."

The assailant's thinking had been patient and thorough all right, Alex reflected, but it was like the thinking of a crabbed, twisted mind. Why drive off a half-dozen horses and leave plain sign, inflict senseless mutilations on the animals, lay up to take a shot at a man's horse and afterward fade enigmatically away?

Somehow the only explanation, a retaliation by some wronged settler, seemed unsatisfactory. Even Jonathan's usual bluster was absent as, after dispatching his crippled mount, he doubled up with Alex and the three men headed back for headquarters.

In the days that followed, Jonathan and his ranch were the brunt of one savage depredation after another. Until now his cattle had sometimes simply dropped from sight, rustled, or were found butchered for the meat and hides. Now time and again their carcasses turned up by the dozen, shot for no apparent reason and left to rot for buzzard bait. One day the crew might have to disperse in several directions to smother several grass fires that had suddenly, mysteriously started at the same time in different places. The next night they would have to rouse out to wet down a blazing shed, with never a sign of a prowler.

Jonathan was shot at twice again, or rather shot close to; there could be no doubt he was the object of this weird war of nerves. Once his horse was killed under him while he was riding home from town at night. Another time he was caught out on the prairie and pinned for two hours in a swale by a hidden marksman located on a nearby ridge.

Again and again Chino took up the track of the elusive enemy, but with no success. He had a fair idea, from what sign he found, of the man's size and build; the tracks of his horse were also distinctive; and always, to all appearances, he worked alone. This was all Chino could learn. The man handled himself with a wily ease that put Sheriff Lou Mapin, who lent his services with equal futility, downwind of a notion.

"I figure he's a professional, Buck," he observed. "There's men who hire out for the cattle wars who ain't regular 'warriors'. They're pure assassins and they work alone. They come as a drummer or a grubline drifter or suchlike, all unsuspected, to size up the situation. Or maybe not a soul will see 'em till they're ready to strike. Well, I would say this boy of yours has been about. He's done this kind of thing before."

"You saying he's been hired?" Jonathan scowled. "The Bittercold bunch, by God."

"Don't jump all that fast," Mapin cautioned. "Not without proof. There's a lot don't make sense, even if I got this bugger pegged right. A killer of that stripe don't play with a victim. He's a professional who plays it safe as he can, and he finishes the job clean as a whistle. I take it this fellow is in no rush. He had made a game of it and has took some long chances doing so."

The "game" was clearly getting under Jonathan's skin. His surly ways worsened. Where he had once roared, he began to snap, his temper fraying more with each fresh assault by a lone, wraithlike enemy, an enemy he couldn't touch.

His outbursts fell on the hapless crew, the loyal core of which was the group of ex-slaves he'd shown the way to manhood and who had stuck by him through the years. Inevitably his insults acquired a highly personal tinge that no man worth his salt could swallow long. For these were proud men; Jonathan had given them a pride to live for, and till now the admitted racism in his affectionate roaring at his "God damn burheads" had been stingless. Remarks like "Christ, next you niggers will get the notion if you take on white airs a spell, the color will rub off," were something else.

Men who had built homes and raised families on the ranch began to quietly pack and depart. The ones who stayed, men who had made the Trask crew the envy of every rancher in the country, went about their work with a sullen, almost ugly indifference. The solidarity that had welded together the GT people like a family was ended. An essential something in the Trask empire, something that couldn't be measured in money or herds, was gone. Everybody at GT was glumly aware of the change.

Then there was all the trouble with Cort. The signs of his drubbing at the hands of Struther Cady had faded to a faint limp and a few yellowish-green bruises, but the undercutting of his pride had left him raw where it didn't show. Even Jonathan was no longer a drag on his wildness; he went on one mad escapade after another, always involving whiskey and women, always leading to brawls and jail. Jonathan no longer listened to Alex' warnings; he defended Cort with a stubborn fury, putting up bail money and paying for all damages.

Alex, just to get away from things awhile, went to Katytown alone one Saturday when nobody else did.

After completing a few minor errands, he loitered along the street. Almost at once he spotted the Cadys' big freight wagon; it was drawn up in front of Old Montrose's store, just as he had first seen it the day he'd helped JoAnne Cady extricate it from a mudhole.

Alex sauntered over by the wagon and took up a careless stance leaning against the hitchrail. Not that he was really curious, but he wondered if the girl were in town today. He could hear Rufus Cady's voice from inside the store. He was commencing to feel pretty foolish standing there, when Cady came out of the store toting a heavy crate which he heaved into the wagon bed.

Straightening, he gave Alex a civil nod. "McKenna. My girl told me how you helped her that time. I'm beholden."

Alex hesistated only a moment before mentioning the campaign of terrorism against Jonathan by a mysterious loner. Cady hadn't heard about it; he seemed genuinely disturbed by the news, and more so on learning that Jonathan believed someone had hired the man to dog him, and that it was probably some of the Bittercold bunch who had sent for him.

"What do you think, McKenna?"

"I don't know what to believe," Alex said truthfully. "But I don't believe anything of the sort was arranged with your knowledge. I told Buck so."

"But some of my kin might of taken action without me?"

Alex did not reply, and Cady shook his head. "I don't reckon. I give the ones I figured was helping themselves to Trask cows some harsh warnings. I figure what I said taken pretty good. But I'll put my ear to the ground and see if I can learn something. You be in town a week from today, I'll let you know what I found."

Alex gave Cady a hand loading the supplies he had purchased into the wagon. Afterward, he stood watching Cady drive away, his thoughts sober. He had liked this man from the first and knew that under different circumstances, they'd be friends. Certain that Cady was innocent of any intrigue, he was determined to see that Jonathan's temper-bleak suspicions brought no harm to the man or his family.

Alex did not start home till late in the afternoon, timing his arrival for supper hour. When he rode into headquarters, woodsmoke was curling from the chimneys of the still-occupied cabins along the creek; a faintness of talk reached him, and a drift of laughter.

A sudden depth of loneliness that shocked him welled high in Alex McKenna. Half the men on the crew had wives and children while he, busying himself over the years with Buck Trask's responsibilities, had hardly had time to think of any life for himself. Not yet thirty, he was in a deadly rut of habit which, because of the demand it had placed on his energies, had never seemed a rut.

A discontent sharper than any he'd known was gnawing in him as he rode to the corrals. Then he forgot it, seeing Jonathan pacing back and forth by the corral gate, the cigar between his teeth in shreds. That was a sure symptom of his temper, and Alex could only wonder what now.

Jonathan gave him a red-eyed look. "You see Cort on your way in? Li?"

"Should I have?"

"All the crew that should be in is in but them, and I warned Cort his work ain't to take him over a mile from here."

"That was days ago," Alex observed. "With Cort, a message like that one bears repetition. You should have left Chino in charge of him after you got back, too. But then that didn't do much good while you were gone, did it?"

Jonathan stared at him. "That's almighty sharp talk, boy. What the hell's eating on you?"

Alex said, "Nothing, forget it," and set about turning in his horse. Finished, he joined Jonathan by the gate again. "We might as well go eat. You won't hurry anything standing about here."

"He ain't back in an hour, I'm sending men out to find him," Jonathan muttered. "Wait. Someone coming there."

Two horses came into sight from beyond the walnut grove. Cort's horse and Liam's too, but only Cort was mounted, his fist clenched around a leadrope. A body, inert and loose and lifeless, hung bellydown across Liam's saddle.

Cort pulled up before them. His eyes were dark-pitted, and his mouth worked blindly. Then he choked out, "It was them Cadys done it, Buck. Them Cadys killed Li."

16

THEY WERE PUTTING OUT ROCK SALT AS BUCK had ordered when he and Liam had come on the clear sign, Cort said. A trail had been broken through the brush where somebody had pushed a small bunch of cows along the creek bank, moving upstream.

The track was too plain to resist following, so the two of them had taken up the trail at once. It ran steadily northeast, and unlike the other cattle thefts, the track did not peter out. Soon they'd come on a barranca where the steers had been butchered for the hides, their raw carcasses left in the dry gully.

From there Cort and Li had followed the trail of the lone horseman to the Cady ranch. Cort had reasoned that the hides were hidden in one of the outsheds, and after reconnoitering to make sure they wouldn't be seen, they had stolen in for a closer look. They had uncovered the fresh hides under some cordwood in the first shed they searched.

Cort had promptly gone to the house and yelled for Rufus Cady to come out. He did at once, his son Struther too, and both of them had gone for their guns the instant Cort made his accusation. In the exchange of fire, the Cadys were driven back into the house, but not before Li had taken a bullet in the chest.

He was hard hit, coughing blood, as Cort got him

back to their horses. They headed back for the GT, but within a half-mile Li had fallen from his saddle. He was dead in less than ten minutes.

Jonathan said not a word as Cort talked. He stood by Li's mount, listening, his face strangely wrenched, and now and then brought his big fist down against the cantle. When Cort finished, Jonathan whirled on him.

"Why'n't you come back here soon's you trailed them beeves to Cady's? Why'n't you fetch me?"

"Buck—"

"I'd a-gone in there with twenty men and cleaned out them rawhiding bastards, and Li'd be alive now."

Alex saw the agony seared into his face, a driven wildness that was more than raw grief; a tension and inheld rage were finding focus too in this moment, exploding with all the feral bigness of his nature.

"Li'd be alive. I'll talk to you later," Jonathan added with an abrupt and terrible calm, his eyes fixing Cort like gunmuzzles. "Right now there's a job to be done."

Alex did not even try to remonstrate with him—not then. In fifteen minutes the whole crew was in saddle, riding out in a body toward the Bittercold range. Jonathan rode ahead of them all, his chin like a bearded crag; his face was iron-like in the fading light of day. He never looked to left or right, and finally Alex, riding nearly at his side, edged over to his stirrup.

"Buck. Don't do this."

Jonathan's stare seemed to go through him.

"I talked to Rufus Cady in town today," Alex said. "He didn't know about anybody being hired to gun you, and he promised to look into the matter." Still Jonathan said nothing and Alex tried again, a desperation crowding his words, "Buck, look, anybody could have planted those hides on Cady's place. Doesn't it strike you as strange that trail was so clear?"

"It don't matter," Jonathan said meagerly, "if some-one planted a thousand hides. Cady killed Li. Him or that whelp of his did. I'm going to string'em both up, and let the buzzards plant 'em."

"If Cort hadn't gone and—"

"They opened fire first!"

"That's what Cort claims," Alex said dryly. "Any-body who's met both Cady and Cort and doesn't happen to be Cort Trask's brother just might not buy that for a moment. On the other hand, I wouldn't put it past Cady's son to fire first, but I'm sure his pa would keep the boy in check."

"That's a fancy guess to make Cort a liar on!"

"One thing I needn't guess about Cort, whether he were right or wrong. He'd tell about anything that happened so he was put in the right. And," Alex said deliberately, "you know damned well he would."

A deadlock of silence stretched between them, then Alex burst out, "Buck, for God's sake—do you want to hang?"

"I stretched plenty of cow thieves' necks and still got my own."

"Those were different circumstances, and you'll find out what the difference is if you go through with this—"

Alex talked on, but he might as well have talked against a blue norther. They were getting close to Cady's, and he began to wish he'd ridden to Katytown to fetch Lou Mapin. But then, what could Mapin have done?

The westered sun was livid at their sides and backs; the day was retreating fast, but there was enough light to show a rider coming across the brow of a hill ahead. Instantly, spotting them, the horsebacker switched course, wheeling away to the northwest.

Jonathan issued a flat order to Chino Lucero and another crewman, in the same moment that Alex made

out the rider's wind-blown skirt and yelled, "Buck!—
tell 'em not to shoot! It's a woman."

"Head her off," Jonathan told them. "Bring her back
here."

Chino and the Negro rider cut in a straight line
toward a point well ahead of the woman. Before they
intercepted her, she had veered due north. She rode
ahead of them for a while, but it was a matter of a
minute or two before they overhauled her.

Jonathan grimly held his men where they were,
waiting. Shortly the three reached them, Chino and the
other flanking the girl. It was JoAnne Cady, her eyes
bright with anger; she was riding like a man and her fair
hair was more disarrayed than ever.

"I seen her before," Jonathan muttered. "Couldn't
say when."

"In the courtroom a few weeks ago," Alex said.
"Cady's daughter."

"That right? Your pa know you're out, Missy?"

"He knows. He didn't like it, but I told him I was
going to town for the sheriff, like it or not." She jerked
at the reins Chino was holding. "You'll let me go if you
know what's good for you."

"Now I'm scared," Jonathan grunted. "If your pa
don't want a sheriff, and I can see why a cow thief
don't, why you fetching one?"

"My pa's no thief." Her eyes were a blue steady
blaze; she pulled sharply at the reins again. "He knew
as soon as one of your brothers was hit in that
shoot-out, you'd be coming to our place, just like you
are. Him and Struther won't budge a step off it, they're
waiting for you, but I got no foolish man pride. I'm
fetching the sheriff!"

"You was," Jonathan said. "You better come with
us." Abruptly he reined forward, and the others put
their horses in motion behind him. JoAnne Cady rode

at the rear, helplessly holding her pommel, Chino's grip firm around her reins. After a minute, Alex fell back beside her.

"I tried to talk him out of it, Miss Cady."

"Oh, you did." She looked at him in wild appeal. "How hard did you try? Can't you do something? Why didn't *you* go for the sheriff?"

"Because if he could get there in time," Alex said slowly, "it wouldn't change a thing. Except one, and I don't want Lou Mapin's death on my hands."

She moved her head in disbelief. "No . . . you don't mean that. He wouldn't kill no sheriff."

"Likely not," Alex said bitterly, "if Mapin came too late. Then Buck would likely give himself up—he believes he can get off easy. But if Mapin got there before he does your pa and brother any harm, and Mapin tried to stop him . . ."

JoAnne was still slowly shaking her head, but he could see she believed him. She whispered, "You know that, don't you?"

"I know him."

"Please." She leaned toward him, a horrified pleading in her eyes. "Stop him somehow, can't you? Please try."

Alex did try. He could only rehash every argument he had already pushed, but he made a running harangue of it till he saw he was merely jogging Jonathan's temper to a tighter boil. Then he desisted.

Sunset made a spreading stain of gold-red as they came into first view of the Cady ranch. It was a hardscrabble place on a griddle-flat plain dotted by a few blackjack oaks. Even the comparative newness of the peeled-log buildings and the tidy look of the yard could not disguise the rawhide poverty or the pride it had nurtured rather than beat down.

No sound came from the house; nothing moved

behind the windows. The whole place looked quiet, almost deserted, except for a few horses stirring in the corral. Jonathan raised his hand for the others to halt, then set his jaw and rode in alone between the buildings. Suddenly he careened his horse to a stop, roaring, "Cady, you got plenty gall holding on here, but it won't get you a thing. Save a sight of trouble and give up."

Cady's voice lifted at once in reply; he was inside the shelter of a trackshed. "You got nerve your own self, Trask. That's why I ain't cut you in half yet. But turn your men and get out o' here or I will."

Jonathan spoke quietly in the clean silence: "Go to hell and shoot, you murdering bastard."

He turned his mount with contemptuous unhaste, then idled back to where his men waited. He gave swift orders that took them out of their saddles and sent them fanning out on the run around the outbuildings, surrounding them. At the same time, not trusting Alex, he had Chino relieve him of his pistol and left a man to watch him and the Cady girl. Jonathan himself joined his men, motioning them to close in on the outbuildings. They knew which shed Rufus Cady was in, but his son might be stationed elsewhere.

Then somebody fired a rifle. It might have been Cady or his son, or one of the GT men Alex couldn't spot. The way things were breaking, it didn't matter a lot who opened the shooting. That single shot rang in brief isolation; then the gunfire broke out in earnest.

In seconds it was apparent that the Cadys had forted up in separate sheds set well apart so that rooting them out would prove a bitter job. No matter what approach the GT men took, they were exposed to the rifle of one Cady or the other; several times a hapless runner was caught in the crossfire. This much was clear enough; otherwise it was like any battle, a chaos of unleashed savagery, of powderstink and yelling men and screaming ones.

The end was a foregone conclusion, but still Rufus Cady surrendered only when one of the wild barrage of bullets the GT men had blindly poured into the sheds found his son. A heavy slug went through Struther's right arm, reducing the bone to splinters, and he could not keep the agony of it voiceless. When Rufus realized what had happened, he thrust his rifle out of the shed door and followed it, hands over his head. Struther had no taste for surrender, but reduced to sobbing pain, he had no choice.

Jonathan checked over his men; they had paid a brutal price for his fury. Two of them were cold dead, another would be dead in an hour or less; five had serious wounds of one sort or another. There were a number of minor injuries, Jonathan himself taking a nicked wrist.

"Was it worth it, Trask?" Rufus Cady shouted, the misery and rage in him trembling his voice. "Did you figure we'd just let you walk over us? Was it worth it?—don't ask yourself, ask them—your men. Ask the dead ones too."

Jonathan did not look at him, only turned his head and jutted his beard at a large oak a hundred yards from the house. It stood in ancient, gnarled isolation, like a frozen troll, in the slow twilight that was cloaking the plain.

"Take 'em over there."

"No—no!" The cry was torn from JoAnne Cady, and Jonathan snarled, "Tie up that damn' girl and stuff a gag in her mouth and put her in the house. Get to it."

A couple of riders moved slowly to obey. The girl's cries were muffled, and she was carried away. Alex sat his horse like a man in a nightmare, watching the men pull off toward the big oak. He could see the Cadys side by side under the tree as their wrists were tied and the nooses dropped over their heads; somebody was leading two horses over there. Alex' guard gave him a hesitant look, then left him and headed for the tree so as to miss nothing.

Alex blinked and straightened, coming to his senses. Now the Cadys were being lifted onto the saddles—while he sat here unguarded. He reined over to the nearest horse with a booted rifle on its saddle, and yanked the weapon free of leather. He kicked in his spurs, lunging his mount forward.

The knot of men broke apart as he raced down on them, and the way was clear to the tree where Jonathan was moving behind the horses the Cadys sat, quirt raised.

"Buck—" Alex savagely yanked his horse to a sliding halt with one hand, bringing up his rifle with the other. "Buck, let them—"

He was aware of Chino Lucero coming up on his right like a lean ghost, and twisted a quick glance at him. A shot came, but not from Chino's gun. The Mexican was reaching for Alex' rein when something like an armored fist, unseen, smashed Alex in the shoulder and drove him sideward out of the saddle.

Vaguely he knew that Chino caught him as he fell, then was easing him to the ground on his back. He felt the massive, sledging pain in his shoulder, but set his teeth and held onto consciousness.

"*Amigo,*" Chino was saying, "I'm plent' sorry this happen. It was not me fire. Chino is only mean to stop you before you get yourself hurt, that is all. Then Cort, he shoot."

Cort. A wilderness of pain and rage took hold of Alex, and then he turned his eyes just as Jonathan's quirt fell across the rumps of the two horses. They walked away, and the two bodies hung and kicked. Alex shut his eyes to the sight.

When he could look again, he saw Jonathan coming toward him. The words tore from him with the hoarseness of revulsion: "Get away—keep away from me, damn you!"

Jonathan came to a halt, staring at him, and Chino said then, "I'm think he out of his head."

"The hell I am!" Alex shouted, ignoring the throbbing pain the effort of speech cost. "Get away from me—you too. All of you bastards!"

"Do like he says," Jonathan said quietly.

"He's hurt pret' bad. I'm think—"

"I don't give a God damn what you think. Leave him be."

Chino eased his head and shoulders gently to the ground. Everything began to swim in his vision, but he heard the clear chink of Chino's spurs as he stood up, saying, "I'm go untie the girl. Someone got to see to him."

Jonathan's reply was lost as the red pain surged high, then ebbed into blackness. The next thing he was aware of, as if from a febrile distance, was the noise of riders going away, all but one.

There on his back, unable to move a muscle, his head turned sideways, Alex saw a rider sitting his horse by the dangling, twitching bodies. The man's head was back, a bottle tilted high in his fist; his throat moved. Then he lowered the bottle, and in the dimming light Alex saw he was Cort Trask. Cort saluted the two corpses, then lifted the bottle to Rufus Cady's mouth.

"Have a drink on me, you sorry ol' sonuvabitch—" The liquor splashed darkly off the white beard and spilled down Cady's clothes.

Cort reined back a little then, chuckling to himself in

an inspired way. Now he stretched his arm high, upending the bottle over the heads of the dead men, pouring all the whiskey over them. Afterward he fumbled out a match and scratched it into flame. Alex raised his head an inch; a cry sighed weakly in his throat, and he dropped his head back, watching helplessly.

Cort's hands lifted, cupping the spoon of flame till it touched Cady's whiskers. An aura of blue flame grew around Cady's bristling beard, polishing his stony eyes and weathered face with an eery glow, spreading down to his drenched shirt. Cort's horse began to dance nervously, and Cort pulled back a safe distance, watching in open-lipped fascination as the fire quickly consumed the alcohol and ate into cloth, the blue flames turning to livid orange. Already the blaze was enveloping Cady's head and shoulders, and creeping downward. Struther's liquor-soaked clothes had caught by now, and he too was quickly turning into a human torch.

The last thread of Alex' consciousness was raveling off when, in a kind of blurring remoteness that seemed faraway and faint, he heard a woman's scream. He saw Cort jerk half-around in his saddle, looking backward; then he spurred swiftly away in the growing dusk. For Alex then, the dusk fled into sudden darkness, total and merciful.

17

A WEEK PASSED BEFORE HIS WORLD TOOK ON meaning again. During that whole time, usually unconscious or out of his head, he was dimly aware that JoAnne Cady did what she could for him. Alone she had gotten him into the house, installed him in the big bed that had been her father's, and dressed his wound. She had brought the doctor from Katytown too, she said, but Alex had no memory of that, only of JoAnne always nearby, always tending his needs.

He had the uncomfortable knowledge that he presented the same problems of care as an infant or an invalid, and the idea of cutting such a figure before the eyes of this backwoods girl dismayed him, as if his dignity and literacy had been stripped away with his clothes. Then, wondering how well any soft, effete woman could have done in her place, he felt ashamed of himself. But all the same, now that he was rational he saw to his own private needs, though he was still weak as a half-drowned cat and ran a risk of tearing open his healing wound.

That what had happened had changed the girl did not surprise him. She spoke only when spoken to, and then answered tersely and curtly. The briskness of her manner saved it from surliness, and a sharp woman was better than a sullen one. All the same he felt concern over the change in her. It was some time before he could bring himself to inquire about her father and brother.

"They hung and burned," she said in a flat monotone. "There wasn't nothing I could do. The ropes burned through pretty soon and they dropped to the ground, but they kept on burning. I was a spell getting the fire out, for all I tried, and they was burned so I was hard put to recognize 'em. After I got you inside and fixed you up, I went to town for the doctor and the sheriff. They come back with me. They took Pa and Struther to town for a coroner's inquest. Some of my kin brought them back here and we buried them."

It was the longest speech she had made; behind the deadness of her words, he felt a complex of feelings that held him uneasily silent.

Finally he asked about Jonathan. She knew only that Sheriff Mapin had served a warrant for his arrest, and Judge Sharpe had directed the grand jury to meet at a special term of the first of next month in order to secure a quick indictment.

By the end of another week, Alex could sit up in bed and take solid food, but he felt dizzy and nearly fell when he tried to walk a little. He knew from JoAnne Cady's terse, distant attitude that she'd like to be rid of him, and the sooner the better. He had taken the bullet trying to save her menfolk and she felt obliged to pay the debt in full, but he was convinced that in her mind, though she said nothing, his long association with the Trasks was like an indelible taint.

He didn't improve matters by mentioning that Jonathan had been harrassed for weeks by an unknown assailant, nor by adding that on the day of his death, her father had promised Alex he'd try to learn what he could about those mysterious attacks.

She listened in icy silence, then said briefly, "A Cady's word binds his kin. If Pa says so, it'll be done. I'll do the asking myself."

"Look." Alex said in perplexity. "I didn't bring it up to make you feel obligated—"

"Pa's word was give. It needs to be kept." Without another word she left the room.

Early next morning she rode away from the ranch, setting the team toward town at a brisk clip. She did not return till well after dark. Entering Alex' room, she dropped a pile of newspapers on the bed without a word. He went through them quickly, feeling an unexpected stab of dismay. They were all out for Jonathan's scalp; the Austin papers in particular. Editorials branded him a blood-stained ogre, and a typical headline blared MAN-BURNER HELD FOR TRIAL.

Alex swore, throwing the papers down. "They all play up that the bodies were set afire. That was Cort's doing, not Buck's!"

JoAnne eyed him bitterly. "My pa and brother are just as dead."

"What Buck did was barbarous enough, all right, but they've worsened it to sell papers." Alex went through the tabloids again, scowling. The grand jury had indicted Jonathan Trask for murder in the first degree, while Cort and the GT crewmen who had assisted him had been indicted separately as accessories before the fact. "Not a mention that it was Li's death that set Buck off," Alex muttered. "Not a one."

Standing by the doorway, JoAnne stiffened; her eyes began to smolder. "I suppose in your fancy lawyer's thinking, that makes a difference."

"It might, if it got brought out in a court," Alex snapped. "I don't see a mention here of a word of it getting into the indictment."

"I don't doubt it would of if you'd a been there!"

"The facts would have gotten in, I can assure you. Something less than half of them were printed here as you can read for yourself—if you can read."

An instant after the words left him, he would have given anything to take them back. She watched him a moment, the color ebbing from her face, then she turned slowly away from him, dipping her face away from the lamplight till he couldn't see it fot the cling of shadow. He realized that though he hadn't spoken with calculation, nothing he might have said could have hurt her more deeply.

At last she said almost inaudibly, "I know I don't talk fine. Not like your kind of people. I can read, and I can print a fair hand."

"I'm sorry I said that. Sorry, and more ashamed than I can tell you."

She would not look at him for a while, and then she said quietly, "You got a way of making a body know when you mean it. I believe you're 'shamed right enough. But you thought it or you wouldn't said it."

"You can say a good many things when you want to hurt. It's wrong, but that hasn't often stopped anybody." Alex spoke wryly, and he added, "I was your age, just about, before I learned the first thing about proper speech. It was plain luck that I had that chance. It's not your place to apologize—it's mine for hinting that you have the least thing to apologize for. You haven't."

"How 'bout a gift for talking yourse'f out of corners with that fancy gab? You learn that too?"

Alex decided her tone was tart but mollified. He grinned. "I suppose so."

"Hmf. You want to hear about this fellow who taken shots at your friend Trask?"

"You learned something?"

"Never mind where," she said guardedly. "I made the rounds of some neighbors and I bent a close ear in town, too. Every hear of a man called Tigo?"

"Tigo?" Alex frowned and shook his head. "What's his other name?"

"Just Tigo, they say. He first come around maybe a month ago. He made an offer. But I got to have your word my friends won't get hurt by what I tell you."

"You have my word. What was the offer?"

"My pa wasn't ever told about it. They knew he wouldn't go along. This Tigo said he would see Buck Trask was put out of the way for a thousand dollars, and some of 'em talked it over and thought they might scrape up the cash between 'em. Ever'body hedged when it come to saying whether the money ever got paid over, but I reckon it did." She hesitated, then burst out, "Can you blame them? Most of 'em are good men, but they've got too scared to think! That's your friend Buck's doing. Can you blame them for being scared?"

Alex leaned back on the pillow, saying wearily, "No, I guess I can't blame them," as he let his eyes shut. If Tigo were a professional assassin, why was he playing with his victim like a cat with a mouse? Why would Rufus Cady, a man in whose honesty he still believed, steal GT cattle for their hides and leave a transparent trail? He'd considered the possibility that Cort might have faked the theft himself to retaliate for the beating Struther had given him, but now began to wonder if there were a connection between the assassin's strange behavior and the stolen cattle. Wondering got him nowhere, though.

JoAnne's abrupt words made him open his eyes. "I suppose you'll be goin' to court to defend him—Trask."

"That's what you think, eh?"

"I don't know," she said a trifle sullenly, watching him from the corners of her eyes. "You got a bullet trying to save my kin. T'other hand you have stuck by him since you was kids, folks say, and you took up for him plenty fierce a minute go. Like you can't get off a notion he is God or something."

"I wasn't sticking up for him that way. He was in the wrong, more wrong than I could swallow. But there's always two sides, and the newspapers left his out. That's wrong too." Again he hesitated. "I want you to understand this. My people were killed by some drunken Comanches when I was six. Gideon and 'Liza Trask—Buck's pa and ma—took me in and brought me up like their own. And Buck and I—well, we were different, so different we hit sparks off each other from the first. But this bad leg of mine—I took that saving Buck's life when a wild steer nearly gored him, and that changed things between us. I don't mean we changed; neither of us did, and that's what made it a strange friendship, I reckon. It's been the kind of closeness you see between flint and steel. They can't help rubbing up fire when they come together. Then it's as I told you once before—I never thought Buck was more than half to blame in anything he did. Not until he did what he did—to your pa and Struther. He was riled about Li, but that was no excuse. It's his side of it, but it was no good excuse. Do you understand me, now? Why I've stood up for him in the past—and why I won't any longer?"

JoAnne stood listening; the hardness had gentled out of her young face, and she did not take her eyes from him as she nodded. "I reckon I do, now. Thank you for telling me."

It was not until she had left the room to prepare supper that Alex realized he'd told her feelings of which he'd never spoke to anyone. He thought, *There never was anyone before.* And lay quite still, watching the ceiling, restless with the unexpected thought and not wanting to be.

After cleaning up the supper tray she brought him, he read the newspapers awhile and finally drifted off to sleep.

A sound brought him sluggishly awake. He was lying on his side, and his eyelids twitched in reflex as the light grew strong. Drugged with sleep, he saw through his lashes that JoAnne was bending over the lamp on the commode, turning it up.

She was wearing a long night gown, a poor girl's gown of white sacking; and straightening, she turned toward the bed. The light behind her cutting through the gown limned for one moment the young body, the wiry and almost boyish slimness, the quick leggy grace that was not boyish, no more than the breasts whose round fullness mocked the loose folds of the demure gown. She bent again, above him now, tucking the blankets around his shoulders. He was motionless, but no longer sleepy; he felt the heavy thud of his heart against his arm, and then his heart and time and everything in his world seemed to stop. He turned his head up and opened his eyes.

Her hair was loose, full of tawny tints from the lamplight which smoothly bronzed her face. He raised his hand and wonderingly touched her face, cheek and lips and chin, feeling the sculptured delicacy of arched and hollowed bone beneath, the sharp bloodwarmth under the velvet skin. Momentarily she quivered; then her face turned and twisted to his touch. He said nothing and she didn't, but she murmured in her throat and brought her mouth parted and awkward down to his. His hands were gentle on her shoulders and then, as he felt her warmth and weight grow against his body, became less gentle.

Suddenly she pulled away from him with a quick-muscled yank and came to her feet. Her breasts were rising and falling quickly; she crossed her arms beneath them and rubbed her palms over her arms where he had gripped her. She shivered and said resentfully, "You're a sight stronger than you look." As quickly as it had come, her cool sureness evaporated; she dropped to her knees by the bed and laid her hot cheek against the quilt.

"You can do 'bout anything you want," she whispered. "I'll let you if you say so. But please—don't."

He touched her hair and cheek again, feeling her trembling against his side, feeling the wonder of this seize him. And he smiled: she knew even less about a man than he did about a woman, and he was finding just how little that was.

"It cut me so—when you said that about if I could read," her lips whispered against his neck. "If anyone else had said it, I would of got mad, maybe laughed depending who said it. But from you it just hurt—I can't tell you how much."

Alex stroked her smooth hair, though he felt foolish and awkward. He said his thought: "I'm just shy of thirty. How old are you?"

"That ain't old. I'll be nineteen next month. I don't see it's all that big a difference."

"Maybe not," he said slowly. "But—"

"I'll learn your kind of mannered talk if you want. I will. I'll study every day, every minute I can find to."

"Not that." His smile was sober. "I wanted to say this is for always with me, JoAnne. I'm the one-woman kind of man. When you're young, ten years makes enough difference so I've got to be as sure it's right for you as it is for me."

"My gran'ma married when she was fifteen. My ma wasn't much older. A woman knows. Leastways our women do. There ain't no mistake." She said it just that simply, as if there were no more to be spoken on the matter.

But of course there was, and they talked for an hour, though it was too early to form many plans. Alex' break with the Trasks had freed him for a new future; during his convalescence he'd busied his mind with his old notion of starting a law practice in Katytown. He wanted JoAnne to hold onto her father's ranch; both of them had their roots in country soil, and probably the most satisfying life would be to keep one foot in town, one on the range. But the need for money might upset any definite plans they laid.

"Plenty time to figure out all that," she said at last. "Time you was asleep."

Alex grumbled, "You sound like a wife already." But he liked it.

18

ANOTHER WEEK HAD GONE BY BEFORE HE WAS FIT for the wagon ride to Katytown. They came in on a Saturday morning, and Alex, usually economy-minded, insisted that JoAnne go to the dressmaker's and have a dress fitted for the occasion. He'd see about getting the judge to perform the wedding that afternoon. First, though, he went to a saloon to enjoy a self-congratulatory drink or two.

The saloon crowd was heavy for a morning, he noticed at once, and there were a number of strange faces. Bending an ear to the talk, he soon gathered that the town was thronged with pilgrims come for the trial which would begin on Monday. There were journalists, the curious, the thrill-seekers, even a tithe of religious fanatics and their ultraliberal foes.

At first so much bustling activity over a cowtown trial puzzled Alex, then he began to realize that the bitter newspaper tirades against Jonathan had merely reflected a rising public clamor. A reforming zeal, reaction against the crime and terrorism that had plagued Texas since the war, had reached proportions of near-hysteria. The time was ripe for the red-eyed zealots to find a focal point for their indignation, and Jonathan, because his lynching of the Cady's had been attended by atrocity propaganda—thanks to Cort's firing the two corpses—made a convenient target.

Almost overnight, Alex was stunned to learn, Jonathan had become the symbol of every barbarism committed since Attila, to whom he was compared by a brassy-voiced journalist from Kansas City. A murmur of lynch talk here and there told as plainly as words that Jonathan Trask would get no fair trial in Katytown. All of Alex' training and personal beliefs told him a man deserved a decent trial, no matter what; and he thought of many things then.

Of the savage action that had sickened him into repudiation of Jonathan and all he stood for. Of what he and JoAnne Cady had found together and how it could be destroyed in this fragile first stage. And knowing behind these things what he must do and why. He stared into his glass, thinking, *You knew it all along, didn't you? All right, go be a damned fool.*

He found Sheriff Mapin in his office in the basement of the courthouse. After a brief exchange of greetings, Mapin inquiring after his health, Alex said, "Lou, the feeling hereabouts is running pretty high."

"That's why I got five special deputies taking county pay. They'll make regular rounds about town every hour till the trial's over. They have orders to break up any assembly that don't look peaceable, keep the people moving."

"Good. Should keep the town from disgracing itself any further. Reckon I could talk to Buck?"

Mapin gave him a careful, rather wondering look, but said nothing as he led the way to the cell block in another corner of the basement. Jonathan was alone in his cell, slacked at complete ease on the narrow cot, and he lounged to his feet as Alex came to the bars. Mapin said, "Sing out when you want to leave," and left them alone.

Jonathan leaned his bulk against the bars; there was a lazy amusement in his dark eyes, and though he'd lost a

few shades of weatherburn from the weeks of confinement, he looked better than Alex had seem him in
years. All the liquor was out of his system; he secmed
alert and completely at ease.

"I was going to ask if you need a lawyer," Alex said
dryly. "From the look of you, you don't need anything."

Jonathan roared. "Well, by God, I knew you had a
bellyful of bein' my conscience. Never figured after
what happened you'd be playin' my angel."

"Why, I guess even God needs his angels. You never
did make much use of a conscience. What I should have
been was your Praetorian Guard."

"What the hell's that?"

"The personal bodyguard of the Roman emperors
who, as the crowds cheered, would whisper. 'Remember, O Caesar, that you are mortal.' I thought a spell in
the calaboose might humble you, though."

"Thought I'd be trying to crawl up a wall myself,
after a week of it. Come to find out, this was what the
doc ordered. Been doing nothing but eat and sleep,
readin' and thinkin'. You know this is the first rest I had
in years? And no hooch, by God. Jesus, I feel like a
million dollars."

"You'll be outfitted for a longer rest than you have
belly for," Alex said grimly, "if you don't get a good
defense."

"Well," Jonathan said somberly, but with his eyes
twinkling, "you know I'd want you standing up for me
in court, boy, but you didn't show up for some reason,
so I sent clear to Austin for a criminal lawyer name of
Hazen."

"You got Lamb Hazen to—? If you want me to
represent your case," Alex said flatly, "get rid of that
shyster. I don't even want his assistance. Drop him."

"Just as you say, boy," Jonathan said agreeably. "I

don't figure nobody's going to get me off altogether."

"Nobody is," Alex assured him. "The least you'll get is twenty years in the penetentiary, and I hope you do. In fact, I want to see to it personally."

Jonathan almost sagged with laughter; finally he said, "Where you been keeping yourself? That straw-hair Cady filly treat you proper?"

Alex felt his face burn. "None of your business."

"Why," Jonathan chuckled, "you God damn blue-nosed Presbyterian, you. Next I'll hear you went and married that big kid." His mood sobered then. "I'm grateful you didn't press no charges against Cort. Shooting you that way. Damn boy. Only why didn't you?"

Alex shrugged. "All I cared about was calling it quits with the Trasks. I didn't want to do a thing for or against any of you—I wanted to cut it clean was all."

"Clean, hell. Welcome back where you belong, boy."

"Don't make a mistake, Buck," Alex said flatly. "I'll stick by you through the trial because what I heard on the street disgusted me. I'll do my best to see you get a square deal—exactly what you deserve, no more, no less. Otherwise I don't feel a lot differently about what happened. What you did to those Cadys was cold murder—I can't find an argument against that fact, and I won't pretend to. You'll plead guilty and, if you're lucky, get a minimum sentence. I hope you don't get a day less."

An hour later Alex was on his way to the GT ranch for the last time. He wanted to collect his belongings and bring them to the hotel in town, for the trial could be long and drawn-out, and he'd want to be next to all that developed. At the last moment, about to confess to

JoAnne that he'd decided to be Jonathan's attorney, he had hedged, explaining that in his quarters at the GT was a good suit that would do to be wed in, and he might as well fetch all his belongings while he was about it.

Slouching on the wagon seat against an angry stitch in his healed shoulder, guiding the team unhurriedly along the road, he let his bleak musings carry to the moment when he could no longer stall off telling JoAnne of his decision to defend the man who'd murdered her father and brother. How could he make her understand that he couldn't do otherwise and justify whatever he lived by, that there was no personality in his position, only duty to a client and to justice? The law, with all its faults, was the mortar that kept human society from flying to pieces. Because he knew just how thin was the civilized veneer over man's raw, war-like instincts, because he feared the unleashing of those instincts, he had made whatever was representative of orderly law into his creed.

He budged his thoughts to the defense he must establish. Jonathan's agreeableness to letting Alex handle everything his way had surprised him. He'd said, "You're the best, boy, and I ain't going to stick at nothing you say," but he had stuck fast at one point. That was when Alex had insisted that, to pare away the aspect of wanton atrocity surrounding the killings, they bring out that Cort, not he, had set fire to the hanging bodies. He was still blindly and stubbornly sheltering his brother, and Alex had given up that argument for the present. A little more friction had occurred when Alex had told Jonathan what little he'd learned about the assassin known as Tigo and then refused, in the face of Jonathan's angry curiosity, to divulge his source.

The GT headquarters was seemingly deserted as he rode in, but he knew from what Jonathan had said that ranch affairs were being conducted as usual, with Chino Lucero in charge. Alex had doubts about his self-control were he to encounter Cort just now, but Cort wasn't around. Samantha answered his knock at the door.

He was surprised to find the parlor floor covered with trunks and crates, and Mercy busily packing them with clothes and other personal things. She looked up as he came in; a gladness touched her face and she came quickly to him and hugged him. "Alex, it's so good to see you. They told me you weren't hurt too seriously . . . but I—I reckon I should of come to visit you."

Alex held her at arm's length and studied her carefully. She was wearing an old dress, her black hair done in a bandanna; behind her gravity he felt something impish, bubbling, irrepressible, the Mercy he remembered from many years ago and whom he'd thought never to see again. That old personality of hers was still subdued like a captive bird, but you could feel it tugging and beating, waiting the moment of release. Even now it flashed in her eyes and quietly animated her small face.

"Why Mercy, you look—" His words floundered, and he weakly motioned at the pile of things on the floor. "What's all this about?"

"I'm leaving, Alex. Leaving the ranch, leaving Texas, leaving—" Her eyes briefly darkened, then sparkled again. "We're going to St. Joe, Samantha and me. I have an aunt there. When all this trouble started, I wrote her and she's agreed to help us. They're moneyed folks, her and her mister, and they can get us started in a dressmaking business or something, show us around to the right people." The rush of her words stopped, and her gaze was level, a little troubled. "Would it sound terrible—I mean with Jon's trouble and all—to say I'm happy for the first time in years?"

Alex shook his head. "Truth is never wrong. If you're happy, more power to you. I'd say you've done your share of penance, if that's the word."

"I hope so." She turned slowly from him, her face lowered. "All that happened—losing the baby, the way Jonathan and me have just been killing off what we felt for each other, all the misery that's been—was God's punishment for what we done to Paul. I'm sure of it—as sure as I am the Lord has pardoned me by showing me this new chance."

Alex said nothing. Mercy's religion was perhaps the only strength she had, and she needed now, as she needed before to use those beliefs in self-castigation, to interpret her blind cry at last for release from her overriding guilt as God's forgiveness. Alex, whose own earliest recollections were tinged with the stark dualities of Scottish Protestantism, understood and sympathized, and thought: *God's will—who knows?*

"I—thought of staying through the trial," she went on. "That would look right, wouldn't it?—and this doesn't. But it's not cowardice, Alex. Everything since the baby died has been a shabby pretense. I have no place with him—he has none with me." She turned fully to face him, and he saw the stir of pain in her face, but it was a pain that belonged to memory only. "What can they really do to him? How can anybody hurt him any more? We was children together, and the children died together—long ago, both of them—on a battle-field at Vicksburg." Her voice sank to a whisper. "They never came back to life or to love. Never, never. A man I didn't know came home to me—and then it turned all dirty, all wrong."

This was how she had talked sometimes in her murmurous, withdrawn periods of self-torture, talked whether there were anyone to hear or not; and Alex saw the anxiety clouding Samantha's face. But the mood passed in a moment; she was the old Mercy again, and she gave him her hand with a soft, bubbling laugh. "Dear Alex—I reckon nobody has to tell you. You always knew things better than anybody."

Alex was only minutes in collecting the clothes, books and other gear he wanted from his old quarters and piling them in the wagon. Then, having said a last goodbye to Mercy and Samantha, he drove back to Katytown.

As he'd expected, a perfunctory check showed that the hotel and several boardinghouses were filled up, but thanks to the generosity of a lawyer friend of his, S. P. Howlitt, he had no difficulty in finding lodging. Howlitt prevailed on Alex to stay with his family as long as he wished. His wife, he added, would like to meet the future Mrs. McKenna.

Alex hadn't been able to locate JoAnne on his return from the ranch; after leaving his belongings at the Howlitts', he returned downtown to cover the stores.

He found her almost at once. She was in Old Montrose's, glancing over some yard goods, and she barely looked up when he said, "When will Mrs. Hoskins have your new dress ready?"

She didn't answer, and he said with a heavy qualm, "What's the matter?"

"Is it true what I been hearing? You're going to defend him anyways?"

Alex knew then he had made a vital mistake in not telling her immediately. Anybody, perhaps one of Mapin's deputies who'd overheard his talk with Jonathan, could have spread the word, and in a few hours it was public currency. There had been no easy way to tell her, but getting it this secondhand way had compounded the hurt for her.

"Yes," was all he could think of to say.

"Ain't that funny? I told myself and I told myself you

was going to say 'no' when I asked. You told me you was through with him and I believed you. I knew what they was saying was only talk and you was going to say 'no'. "It's just so funny."

Alex tried to make her listen; he talked about ethics and conscience, and she cut in across his words with a brittle, dry-eyed coldness: "I won't hear no more from you. Your word ain't worth a thing to me. My pa and my brother are dead. Their bodies was set fire to like a pair of wore-out boots. You find anything to say for the men who done that, you go tell a judge. But don't you ever tell me another lyin' thing. Not ever."

She brushed past him going out of the store. Alex stood where he was, feeling as alone as he'd ever been. The difference was that before, he had hardly ever thought about it. Now he would hardly be able to stop thinking of it.

19

FROM THE BEGINNING, ALEX HAD A FIGHT ON HIS hands. The state was determined to make an example of Jonathan Trask. Not only did the prosecution assemble an array of the sharpest legal talent in the southwest, the district attorney was quietly shuttled to the rear ranks of proceedings, and a special d.a. pro tem, an orator who had delivered the keynote address at his party's last national convention, was appointed in his place by Judge Sharpe, a leading spokesman for the party in power. The enormous cost was footed by the state treasury through a politico-legal maneuver unprecedented in the history of any state—a special appropriations bill was rammed through the legislature.

This fund had also provided transportation and rations for a company of regular militia brought in ostensibly to keep order but actually, it was widely rumored, to prevent an army of "Trask's Niggers" from swooping down on Katytown to free their boss. The rumor was just that, a lie neatly promulgated to keep public opinion incited, the militia being present to give substance to the fear rather than to allay it.

The raw explosiveness of the situation almost decided Alex to ask for a change of venue, but he decided against it. No matter where Jonathan was tried in Texas, the state politicians could bring their influence to bear. Besides the affair had achieved so much notoriety that people across the state were choosing up sides according to their own interests. And in spite of the weight of local sentiment against Jonathan, stirred up still further by state propaganda, a surprising number of citizens estranged by his actions ranged themselves in his favor when the chips were down. Rufus Cady, a Missouri freesoiler and a Union soldier, had been entirely too outspoken on his positions; a man needn't love Buck Trask's guts to side him in this instance. He was still one of them—Cady had been the alien, the outsider, who had ruffled his own share of feathers.

Time and again over the years, Jonathan's business and legal interests had taken Alex to Washington, D.C. and other points East. As often as not he found himself handling a score of favors for other Matheson County cattlemen; people not only liked and trusted Alex, they respected his zest for "impossible" undertakings so much he'd been urged time after time to run for public office. Though loyalty to the Trasks had confined his personal ambitions, Alex' original interests had never flagged. Over the years he'd kept in touch with law school cronies, many of whom had climbed high in legislative and judicial circles.

Now, with Jonathan's considerable fortune at his disposal, Alex drew unstintingly on associates old and new to surround himself with a formidable coterie of legal minds that almost outflanked the prosecuting force.

The first day after court convened were taken up, thanks to the hot division of opinion in the county, by a tedious wrangling over the selection of jurymen. After charges and specifications in the grand jury indictment had been introduced, the prosecution stated that it would show Jonathan Trask had murdered two men in cold blood. There had been nothing at all cold-blooded about the killings, Alex pointed out in the rebuttal by the defense. He meant to hammer at the point that the defendant had been in a highly emotional state. He didn't want to see Jonathan acquitted in any case, only dealt with according to his crime. Since the best defense in the world couldn't have secured an acquittal, he could concentrate without reservation on one goal: saving his client's life.

As the days ground by, the trial settling into a bitter, dragout contest, Alex was satisfied to be holding his own against a powerful adversary. Bit by bit, through success and error, losing a point here and gaining another there, he was building his case and gaining a hard-won wealth of practical experience. But the tension of leading a fight against heavy odds while carrying the daily courtroom grind of issues and personalities was taking a vicious toll of him, mentally and physically.

He became haggard and rundown from a combination of too little sleep and too few meals, these hastily eaten and digested on the run. His nerves were drawn to the breaking point from a constant whirl of work and activity, marshaling evidence and witnesses, arguments and legal opinions, organizing strategy and procedure to a fine degree only to be forced often as not to a hasty retrenching and improvising.

He learned that JoAnne was staying in town at a local boardinghouse, no doubt so that she could follow the trial. He tried again and again, at such odd times as he could spare, to see her and talk to her. She refused to see him, and her indomitable landlady reinforced the edict. Probably for the same reason, she never showed up in court except for a brief hour early in the trial when the prosecution called her as witness to the events leading up to the crime.

Meantime Jonathan rubbed Alex raw on several counts, not the least of which was his monumental cheer in the face of a possible death sentence. It made Alex suspicious and worried. Throughout the trial Jonathan remained almost suspiciously cheerful. He slept well, had his meals catered by the best restaurant in town, put on weight, and despite his imprisonment, cut a figure of ruddy health. He only gave a sad, indulgent little chuckle on learning that Mercy had left him. That grand passion had suffered through too much, grinding down and wearing away till it wasn't worth even a twinge.

The only thing that could upset his cocksure blandness was Alex' repeated insistence that Cort be called to the stand to testify his guilt in the corpse-burning. Jonathan wouldn't budge an inch in his refusal to implicate his brother beyond the charge of accessory already facing him. Nor would any of the GT crewmen who'd been present give testimony against Jonathan's wish. So Alex found, and resigned himself.

Next it came to his ears that Lamb Hazen, the Austin legal counsel Jonathan had agreed to let go, was still around and had visited Jonathan in his cell several times. Alex knew Hazen for an unscrupulous shyster who was still in practice only because he was too shrewd to leave any trail through the quiet webs of his extra-legal chicaneries.

Jonathan insisted that Hazen had only been paying friendly visits, but Alex gave him a flat ultimatum. Either the defense would be handled his way entirely, as agreed, or Jonathan could turn the whole show over to Lamb Hazen. Otherwise he wasn't to see Hazen again or contact him in any way.

Somehow Jonathan's cheery argreement didn't ring quite true, but Alex couldn't smell what, if anything, might be amiss. He had come this far with the case, things were going reasonably well, and he put aside his misgivings and stubbornly set himself to seeing out what he'd begun to the finish. So the trial went on and the weary weeks dragged by.

On the last day, Alex countered the prosecution's summation with a carefully organized analysis of the social, economic, legal, and political motives touching his client's action, couching it all in a rough cow-country idiom his listeners appreciated. He made obscure and complex matters wholly understandable to them, and he was comprehensive. Judge Sharpe kept overruling his sharp attacks on the political machine that was out for Jonathan Trask's scalp, but he success-fully interjected quite a few subtle points that went over the bench's head.

Sweeping the room with his eyes, he caught a good deal of reaction. He mentioned Jonathan's war record, reminded them of the immense debt the country owed Jonathan Trask for his part in making it a decent place to live, and even went so far as to state that many of Jonathan's ways were those of a violent and hardened character, "but not—I repeat, gentlemen—not of an evil man. Jonathan Trask is a product of our times—as much yours and mine as his. When we repudiate his ways, we repudiate our own." To give way to a revengeful passion after the death of his younger brother Liam had been wrong, but the act was neither premeditated nor cold-blooded.

Moreover, though it was Cortney Trask's word against JoAnne Cady's as to who had started the gunfight that ended in Liam Trask's death, it could not be denied the two Trask boys had followed the trail of their stolen cattle to the Cady headquarters. Alex had to force himself to state this part; it was his duty to bring out on his client's behalf every mitigating factor, though he didn't remotely believe Cady had been guilty of either theft or precipitating the fight with Cort and Li.

Later, talking with Jonathan in his cell, he said as much. Jonathan, sitting slackly on his cot, one leg cocked up, only yawned. "That's your duty, boy. You said so yourself."

"Sometimes duty leaves a fairly rotten taste."

"Well, you're dead set in your head against Cort, that's all. Anyway it's all over but the shouting."

"You still could hang. The jury hasn't brought in a verdict yet."

Jonathan waved a hand. "Hell, you talked it up just fine. Most I expect is a stiff term in prison, and Lamb says—"

"Hazen—" Alex pushed away from the wall where he was leaning, dropping his folded arms. "You said you wouldn't see Lamb Hazen again."

"I ain't. We had it all arranged by the time I promised you. Lamb and me went over things start to finish. Thing now, he says, is to get me safe past a noose into the pen. Then he can start things moving for me. In a year, two years, when things have simmered down and the political situation has cooled, Hazen'll ask the state supreme court to review my case. Soon's they grant me a new trial, I should be out in a month."

Alex was speechless for a quarter-minute. He said between his teeth, "What makes you so sure the supreme court'll find grounds for review? If they do, why should they grant a re-trial? And what in the name of hell makes you think a second trial will get you off scot-free? The emotional and political climate will change, but the evidence and testimony against you won't. I want to hear your reasoning."

"Well." Jonathan grinned, and scratched his ear. "You know Lamb. Leastways you say you do. He's got ways of making folks come to taw. If one way don't work, there's always another. I wouldn't be surprised he's got ways he ain't tried yet."

"That's what I know," Alex said thickly. "I wanted to hear you say it. I know his ways. Bribery—blackmail—threats backed by hired thugs."

"Now, boy, you don't know any of that."

"Everybody knows it. The way he works, through other people, nobody can prove it is all."

"Same difference."

"You bastard." Alex could no longer keep the trembling from his voice as he came over to the cot. "Lamb Hazen is only one kind of crook. He has nothing on you."

Jonathan's smile faded. "Look, boy, I never strung you along none. I didn't want nobody but you talking up for me to a home-growed jury. Ain't a soul in these parts don't know you and like you. I needed you to talk me out of a hangrope, and you good as done it. But I ain't going to rot in a prison rest of my life if I can help it. If Lamb Hazen can get me out in a couple years, think I ain't a-going to let him? I said you was running this show, but it's pretty near over. I kept my word, by God."

"No. It was a lie from the start." Alex leaned forward in his intensity. "You and Hazen ran the show. You used me was all, but you planned it so I'd think otherwise. You told me nothing until now because you figured I'd have dropped the case cold if I'd known what would follow."

"Well, God damn," Jonathan said angrily. "You think after how you preached at me all these years, I'd trust you not to cut my throat with you God damn do-good conscience? It ain't your neck on the block, it's mine, and I knew there wasn't nobody but me going to look out for it—"

Jonathan's words had seethed to a roar as he started to his feet, tapping his finger on his chest, but he wasn't fully on his feet when Alex hit him, a full-arm smash to the jaw. The blow knocked him back on the cot and he lay there looking vastly surprised as his mouth bled into his beard.

Jonathan's loudness brought a deputy on the run, and Alex curtly said he wanted to leave. The deputy unlocked the door, and he walked out without another glance at Jonathan.

On the street, Alex' brisk stride slowed; there was a trudging weariness to his steps as he headed for the Howlitt home. *I should have known,* he kept thinking. *I should have known.* He had leaped into this battle with a blind crusader's instinct, and what it had gotten him was a taste of dirt in his mouth. What it had cost him was the largest forfeit of his life—JoAnne.

By midmorning next day, the jury finished its deliberations and shuffled back into the courtroom. Alex sat at the defense table, palms flat on the scarred tabletop, his head bent. The foreman's voice, as he read off the verdict of second degree murder, seemed to come from a distance. So did the drone of Judge Sharpe passing sentence, imprisonment in the state penitentiary for the rest of Jonathan's natural life. Alex would have laughed aloud, but his edge was too dulled for that; anyway what did it matter?

The sheriff came forward to take Jonathan into custody; Alex did not even look at the man he had defended as he rose, gathering up his briefcase and notes. He didn't want to see whatever expression that black-bearded face wore. He walked from the courtroom, pushing through the eddies of people; some of them spoke to him and he didn't hear them. He had done his duty by his client, had won as much victory as he'd worked for, and there was a feeling like death in his bones. All the way from the courthouse to the Howlitt home, he felt like a man sleepwalking.

Mary Howlitt said something to him as he entered

the house; he fumbled out some words and went on to his room. Standing there, looking around him and slowly rubbing his neck, he felt the everyday world wash back into focus around him. He heard a bird outside the window; he saw the flowered pattern of the wallpaper and a sun-square full of lazily swimming motes. A semblance of calm and order came back to things, and he thought wryly, *It's ended, finished, and what's the odds now? That's you all over. You'll be a sight happier when you quit taking yourself too damn' seriously.*

Would that ever happen? He smiled again and shook his head, then got his suitcase from the closet and began packing his clothes. He was surprised at the relief he felt that the long weeks filled with work and strain were over; that was a form of self-escape, he supposed, and so was the sudden urge he felt to get away, to be anywhere but here, to let his nerves quietly stitch up while the broken pieces of his life fell into new patterns and he made plans. At the moment he didn't greatly care what direction things took; he just wanted to get far away, to rest and think.

Mary called from the parlor, "Alex, you have a visitor."

Wearily Alex dropped a fistful of shirts in the open suitcase, then went out to the parlor. Mary brushed quietly past him, leaving the room, as he entered. JoAnne was standing in the middle of the room. She looked taller than he remembered, more slender, and he realized this wasn't only because she was actually thinner, her outdoor tan almost gone. She was wearing a well-cut bombazine dress, fresh and new, the skirt rustling in crisp folds as she turned to face him. She was beautiful, he realized—not conventionally, but handsome beyond mere prettiness, the fine bone structure of her face more prominent, her pale hair pulled to a smooth club back of her neck.

She said slowly, "I was in the courtroom today. I spoke to you when you left—reckon you didn't hear me."

"I didn't see you." For the moment he could only look at her with his thoughts blank; he did not know what else to say.

"I hadn't seen you except at a ways off for—for weeks. I didn't know—" Her voice started to break. "Just look at you—fine public figure you cut—all thin and wore down like you hadn't ate a square meal in—and when you been getting any sleep? Answer me that!"

"Well, I—" Something cleared suddenly away in his mind. "Would that be—that wouldn't be your wedding dress?"

To his consternation she began to cry; he had never seen her even close to tears. "Oh, you—lawyer! You damned, damned lawyer."

"I guess that's right." He smiled tiredly and started a step toward her, but she was in his arms before he finished it.

20

THEY WERE MARRIED THAT SAME AFTERNOON. A day that had started as the worst in his memory ended in a new beginning. And Alex McKenna would often wonder, looking back, why he'd ever thought he was contented in that other life. He choose to remain in Katytown, to raise his family here and make him dream of a law practice a reality.

He and JoAnne divided their time between weekdays at their town house and weekends spent at her father's ranch, now kept up by two hired hands. It was touch-and-go a long while, but they managed to hold onto both ranch and town practice, and by the time Alex was getting more clients than he could handle, the pinch was off.

He was too busy to give more than casual note to the deteriorating affairs of the GT empire. The great ranch that he had called home for more than two decades was of no concern to him now; he was no longer handling its legal business and would have refused any that was offered.

He knew what was common gossip: that Cortney Trask, along with the rest of the GT men involved as accessories in the Cady lynching, had gotten off with a few months in prison. Then word came that Cort was back at the GT, trying to get the tangle of Jonathan's affairs in order. Alex smiled at that. Cort's business sense was on a par with his other talents for judgment. However it was soon learned a battery of good lawyers in Austin was working on the legal and bookkeeping end, while Chino Lucero was as competent a right hand for Cort as he'd been for Jonathan. With attorneys to handle the headwork and Chino in effect running the practical side of things, the ranch could almost take care of itself. Alex guessed that even from pirson, Jonathan was keeping in a guiding hand through his lawyers and Lucero, while letting Cort have the illusion he was doing important things.

But the year 1873 began with uneasy rumors. The golden boom of railroad building that was to have brought civilization and prosperity to the rude frontier collapsed—construction had outstripped the limited needs of a sparsely populated land. There was widespread speculation, loose credit, a stench of graft in the nation's capital, followed by the scandal of the Crédit Mobilier: the bribery of U. S. Congressmen by the railroad interests. Then Black Friday—the nation's finances crumpled, and banks toppled like dominoes.

Overnight, cattle prices dropped to rock bottom. Many big ranchers with herds of unsold cattle on hand and money tied up with the ruined banks, were wiped out completely. Thanks to adroit maneuvering by the Trask attorneys, an alert ear to whispers on the financial winds, and hasty selling, some of Jonathan's fortune was salvaged though nearly all his interests were gotten rid of at a loss.

Alex shared with other Texans a concern over the course of affairs for his state, county and community. His concern did not scale to anxiety simply because his personal affairs, wife and home and a successful practice, occupied his life so fully. Then, by fall,

Robert Gideon McKenna was born, and he was too lost in the pride and pleasure of fatherhood to pay very much attention to any outside matters.

Meantime Lamb Hazen and his associates hadn't been idle. They were testing for a review of Jonathan's case by the state supreme court. They came up with a contention that Rufus Cady's ranch headquarters where the lynching had occurred was just across the Lawton County line; therefore, on the grounds that Judge Sharpe's Matheson County court had lacked jurisdiction in the case, a mistrial should be declared. Admittedly the line had always been in doubt; now the surveyors of both counties went to work and discovered that the line did indeed run a hundred feet south of the tree where the hanging and immolation of the two men had occurred. The supreme court undertook a review and soon announced that the Trask case would be retried in Lawton County. Not long afterward rumor had it the Trask ranch had sold a herd of a thousand prime three-year-old steers to each of the two county surveyors for next to nothing.

Simultaneously with release of news of Jonathan's impending retrial, the GT ranch was shaken by a new wave of terrorism. The depredations by the mystery man called Tigo had ceased on the day Judge Sharpe had sentenced Jonathan to prison for life. Now, a year and a half later, the gadfly was back in the bull's flank. All the earmarks of the one-man terror who had previously plagued the GT were there, but he was no longer satisfied with making the bull grunt and tail-swish at a stinging irritant here or there.

Now his strokes fell bold and swift and savage, one after the other. Mysterious fires were set everywhere; droves of cattle were found dead, massacred by bullets or driven in bunches off canyon rims. Men, too, fell prey to an unerring marksman, always hidden, who shot never to kill, always to incapacitate. These bites were deep and vicious; the gadfly was striking for the heart now, and all the bull could do was stomp and bellow his fury.

Already in a bad way from the '73 panic, the Trask fortune was practically bone-picked to dredge up funds for Jonathan's new defense. Soon it was learned the situation had become so serious that the GT was borrowing heavily against the collateral of its various holdings, even its remaining herds.

By now all but a few of the old crew, the colored cowboys and their families who had once formed the proud nucleus of the Trask pride and power, had left. They were replaced by hard-bitten men who worked for wages, not ordinary punchers but "warriors" whose knowledge of cattle and range was incidental. Bands of these men, well-armed and well-mounted, were out by day and by night, seeing to the safety of ranch property while they kept on the hunt for the elusive Tigo. Such men came high, and their value proved negligible. If their vigilance forestalled some acts of terrorism, Tigo was never at a loss for fresh diversions, hiting unpredictably at any time, any place, in any way that suited him.

None of which held any interest to Robert Gideon McKenna or his proud, delighted parents as they watched him, plump and crowding, taking his first steps.

Howlitt and some of Alex's other friends had prevailed on him to run for the state senate next term. After accepting the draft, Alex felt obliged to follow all important legislative and judicial actions. He was one of the first to hear about Jonathan's new trial, and he followed events closely through the winter of 1874—75. Hazen and others were preparing their briefs, and pretrial wrangling was becoming keen. The trial was set for late March.

On a quiet spring evening Alex sat in his parlor after supper trying to concentrate on a newspaper. At first he thought his noisy son was the reason he couldn't bring his attention to focus, but when JoAnne ended Robert Gideon's romping exuberance by putting him to bed and Alex still felt disoriented, he told himself it was ordinary spring restlessness. Finally, chin on his chest and scowling at his unlighted pipe, he admitted the truth to himself.

Glancing at his wife beside him on the sofa, he permitted himself a moment's satisfaction just watching her. He remembered with pleasure the girl she had been; he saw with deeper pleasure the woman she had become, the young serenity of her face and the fullness of maturity, deep-breasted and round-hipped. Her hair was done in a smooth, pale-gold bun with a silver clasp; she was wearing simple calico now, fashionable and fitted, and sometimes she wore bombazine and silk. She made her own clothes, but someday she would order them made and see to their making with the same care and taste, he knew. The housekeeper and maid who might someday do her bidding would never, for all Jo's supervision, be able to order a household better than JoAnne herself. As a hostess, she was a match for the peerless Samantha who had presided for so long over the Trask home.

For such matters, it seemed, she had almost an instinct; reshaping the speech habits of a lifetime had been far more difficult. She had learned grammar quickly, but had worked long and painfully to incorporate rules of diction into her everyday speech. She did everything because she wanted to; a Cady woman did properly by her man, she had told him seriously. Alex, a little awed by her accomplishments in a few short months, hadn't needed to remind himself that these were small things beside the rest, the love and respect and character that came first, but he was proud of them.

"Jo"—he laid aside his pipe and waited for her to look up from her darning—"I've been thinking. Reckon I'll ride over to Saba City tomorrow."

Saba City was the county seat of Lawton County; with Jonathan's trial opening day after tomorrow, there was no need to ask his reason. But she said, "Is it professional interest, Alex, or just curiosity—or what?"

"Partly the first and mostly the second," he said wryly. "It's been two years and six months, Jo. I'm wondering what that long in prison's done to a man as arrogant as he'd become. He spent two years in a Union stockade, but he was younger then and he still believed in something."

"Himself," JoAnne said quietly. "From all you've said, I doubt he ever believed in anything else, and did he ever lose that belief?"

"That's a point," Alex admitted. "Call it a variance in perspective, then—the world looked a lot differently to him once. Then it all turned dirty."

"With his help."

"Yes. Jo, I don't say he hasn't deserved all that's happened to him nor that he deserves to go free now, as he possibly will. It doesn't seem likely, but never underestimate Lamb Hazen. He's a conniver and a crook, but he's also a gifted orator and a hell of a brilliant lawyer. Suppose he gets Buck off—what then? What does he come home to? A ruined ranch, a mass of debts, a slew of people with old grudges, an enemy whose face he doesn't even know, and not a soul in the world that gives a damn—"

"Doesn't he have a brother—Cortney?"

"His last living tie. A weakling who's watched the ranch left in his charge fold up and die. Maybe no man could have saved it, but only a weakling would fold up along with it. But that's Cort for you. He came into Katytown two weeks ago, took a room in the hotel, crawled into a bottle and hasn't climbed out since. It's common talk. He's not self-blaming, understand, just self-pitying. And this, my dear, will prove the unkindest cut of all—Buck set more store by that boy, God knows why, than anything else. Except for one girl long ago. He'll never come home to nothing, Jo—he'll come home to a good deal less than that."

"Doesn't he deserve to?" Her face held a suggestion of the bitter tension he remembered too well. "Doesn't he deserve nothing and less?"

"I don't know," Alex said slowly. "Maybe. It depends on how much judgment you want to lay. Whether you don't feel that somewhere, sometime, a man's debt is paid, and any hardship wished on him from then on is wanton revenge."

"Oh—then if you've stopped judging him, are you judging me now?"

"Only myself," he said soberly. "I didn't lose a father and brother at his hands, Jo. I can't touch by a country mile what you've felt. Only . . . I think of what you and I have had together. And we have Robert Gideon. All of it a kind of happiness that Buck Trask was never permitted to know. Don't mistake me—I'll never take up with him or for him again. But if a man's alone, suffering, and you once called him friend—it ought to be worth a kind word, an outstretched hand, if nothing else."

"Alex . . ." Her eyes softened. "You're always so—not free and easy, you have that stiff-necked Scot's eye for good and evil. But so ready to return good for harm. So strange to think . . . do you remember that day the trial ended and I came to you—finally?"

"Every detail. I always will."

"It's ironic, I guess. I'd thought I hated you because of your loyalty to Jonathan Trask—and then that day, in court, seeing you worn to a shadow of yourself, all for a principle—I started loving, really loving you. Till that hour, I was a little girl playing at romance." She stood and placed her hands on his shoulders, and bent to kiss him. "You see, I do understand you after my fashion. And I'm proud, very proud, that you're so much more than I can ever be. Go to Saba City and be as much Samaritan as you want. And I'll try—for your sake—not to hate him any more."

21

"Is like old times," Chino Lucero said, and added predictably, "Haaah."

Chino never changed. Now, as always, he simply watched life go by with a detached, clownish amusement, not caring much how things went. And as always, his lazy loyalty to Jonathan was the only thing that could remotely regulate his careless comings and goings.

He and Alex and Jonathan were a night and day out of Saba City, riding south, and by now they were touching the vast north range of GT's holdings.

The dry grass bent under the wind; a few curlews took wing overhead, going north to their nesting grounds. The sedgegrass plain with its mottes of liveoak and pecan rolled unmarred, changeless, to every horizon, as it had since Alex' earliest remembrance. He sharply remembered another spring day when he and Jonathan had ridden from the north across this same stretch, a day identical to this in more ways than one. Then too, Jonathan Trask had been coming from a prison to a nearly impoverished homeland. But that had been a younger Jonathan, a youth bursting with hope and plans, his muscles still untried. Even if that day's bright promise had soon proved hollow, there had been the hope, the belief; and Alex thought, *Lord in heaven, was that ten years ago?* It was, almost

204

to the day. Well, one thing to be said for all that had happened, good or bad, in those years—there had been hardly a dull moment.

And (somehow it rubbed him against the grain) Jonathan, whatever scars he might carry out of sight, had come off outwardly unchanged. If he'd once looked older than his years warranted, he now seemed younger, for he didn't appear to have aged a day since Alex had last seen him. Often enough over the years, he had been worn and haggard from driving himself, and heavy drinking had never helped. Not that Alex had expected the penitentiary to break Jonathan's spirit— he knew better than that—but it didn't seem quite right for him to come out unscathed, bursting with health and vigor, vital even in the taut bite of his familiar cynicism.

"I'm surprised," Alex had finally felt obliged to remark. "You're looking in fine shape."

"Outside work," Jonathan had explained carelessly. "Good behavior. Spent most of my hitch on the prison farm." He had eyed Alex critically. "You put on a little weight, but you always could of stood some. Married life 'pears to agree with you."

Outside work, Alex dourly reflected, only partly accounted; a man without much of a conscience, lacking even the external one Alex had once provided, didn't spend time brooding on his sins. What did surprise him was Jonathan's air of indiffernt calm, with the empire he'd built on sweat and other men's blood drifting toward wholesale ruin. Probably the buoyancy he felt at coming home again a free man let no obstacle look too large to hurdle.

Alex was coming to the wary conclusion that his trip to Sara City had been a fool's errand—two weeks away from his work and family wasted on a man who needed nobody. The fact that of his old circle only Alex and

Chino Lucero had come to the trial had produced from Jonathan no particular reaction except a flash of bitter irritation that Cort hadn't bothered to show up.

Typically, though, he had brushed aside Alex' blunt warning of just how far Cort had fallen: "Ain't seen him your own self, have you? Thought not. Hearsay's cheap. If there's anything to it, I'll snap Cortney back to time fast, you bet."

All Alex cared about was getting home to JoAnne and his son. After two weeks of a hotel bed and hotel grub and hours on end in a courtroom watching Lamb Hazen's incredible machinations unfold, he was tired and fed-up. It had been outside the courtroom, when the hours were late, the bottles were low, and tongues were loose, that he had really learned about the devious bends of Hazen's strategy. Jonathan hadn't said a word one way or the other, but Alex knew he'd nearly exhausted the remainder of his fortune paying out massive bribes at Hazen's direction. A heavy price to pay for even freedom, but Lamb had earned his exorbitant fee.

Lawton County people were cattle people. When Lamb Hazen had thundered, "Because one man dared a bold action that served a warning to all potential thieves, the cost of trouble and bloodshed was spared to many," they'd listened. When he'd heatedly declared that "by the Cadys' violation of the Lord's own commandments, 'neither shalt thou covet' and 'neither shalt thou steal,' they brought on their heads a retribution that I say—and bedamned to the mockers of justice who will decry my words—was richly merited," they'd nodded grimly. At the conclusion, when Judge Smyte had promptly discharged the prisoner with "Get the hell out of here, Buck. Time for you to set up drinks over at the Longhorn," they had cheered.

Things couldn't have gone more smoothly, and Jonathan had some small reason for his ebullience, but his mood was wearing thin at last as they rode deeper into GT range now.

The effects of the terrorist's lone-handed carnage were plain on every side. Vast stretches of burned grass cut blackened swaths across the prairie, and several times they detoured so that Chino could point out the clean-picked bones of dozens of cattle killed off one way or another.

It was Alex who first spotted the trickle of smoke lifting above a motte over southeast. The sun was in his eyes, and he tugged his hatbrim down to shade them, and then was sure. He was about to speak when Jonathan and Chino spotted the smoke simultaneously. All three of them reined in with a common thought.

Jonathan said, "Any of our men working over this range now?"

"I'm not know," Chino shrugged. "I'm leave Malachi in charge. I'm not give him any orders, I'm tell him handle things like he want. But I'm got plent' doubt this is fella cause alla trouble."

"Why?"

"We ain' come near catch him at anything. This one smart fella. Every time we find cow kill, fire set, it is long after he come an' gone. He is never letting us get close. This fire, you see, she's just got started."

"Let's get over there," Jonathan snarled, and quirted his animal into a run.

But a caution blunted his haste before he reached the motte; his companions caught up with him, and the three of them advanced slowly into the trees.

In the center of a small clearing they found the fire. It was untended and smoking badly, and there was nobody around. No accouterments of campsite or branding job were to be seen. There was nothing, in fact, but the smoldering pile of twigs and branches, plainly lighted only minutes ago.

The three men sat their horses in silence, studying the sun-mottled stillness of thickets and trees on every side. There was not a breath of wind, not a movement or a sound, only the heat and drowsing leaves and utter quiet. "Haaah," Chino whispered hoarsely. "We are ducks on the sit, I'm think."

Alex had the same feeling. The heavy verdure around them could hide one man or a regiment of men. Obviously the situation—even to a heaping of green wood to make the fire smoke—had been contrived to pull them in here. But for what reason?

Chino's horse tossed its head and whickered suddenly. At once, from a shield of greenery to the right, came a horse's low whickering answer. Instantly Jonathan wheeled his mount with a heavy hand on the reins; his other hand stabbed to his holstered Colt.

"I wouldn't, Mr. Trask. There is a rifle trained on your heart." The words were followed by a soft laugh like ice tinkling.

Jonathan's hand froze; his glance raked the thickets. There was nothing that Alex could see, not a shadow of a presence; yet the voice and laugh had a startling nearness. And Alex thought, *That laugh—I've heard it at one time or another, but where?*

"Discard your guns, gentlemen. Pistols and rifles, and one at a time. You first, Señor Lucero," the voice went on gracefully. A pause as Chino flipped his gun out gently and tossed it to the ground. He slipped his rifle from its scabbard and dropped that too. "Next Mr. Trask . . . now you, Mr. McKenna."

"I'm not packing one."

"Ah, always the pacific one, sir. You may descent,

gentlemen. Keep your hands in sight, please, and step away from your horses."

Each word was a velvet threat, and the three men wordlessly did as they were told. Jonathan growled then, "Where the hell are you? Time you showed your slimy face."

"Behind you, Mr. Trask. I am Tigo."

They all turned their heads. A wiry figure of a man was standing under a large oak. He held a rifle leisurely trained. Alex had last glanced that way only seconds before, and there had been nobody.

The man wore black. His heat broadcloth suit, and low-pulled Stetson were dead black; his tall jackboots were a shining black. A mask of black silk, a dandy's bandanna, covered all his face but the faint slit between his hatbrim at brow level and the bridge of his nose where the mask ended. A breeze fluttered the light silk, but the face remained hidden. There was a theatricality to this whole pose, Alex thought, but the chill it sent up a man's backbone was real. Maybe it was the eyes, palest gray even in shadow, eyes cold as death. And he knew.

"Danziger," he said.

Jonathan clipped a glance at him. "Danziger?—the hell. The Pig's in his grave eight, nine years." He scowled. "His way of talkin', though, puts a man in mind—"

"Not Alvah, Buck. His brother. Lat."

The man in black gave his light, graceful laugh. He moved slowly forward now, holding his left leg rather stiffly. He tapped it with a bony finger. "I can still hinge the knee only with difficulty. Legacy, Mr. Trask, of that tender moment when you closed your cunning trap on my headstrong brother some years ago. The bone was shattered to splinters—beyond repair by the finest surgeon, and as it was, I received something less than solicitous surgical care. This, however, remains of small moment next to a further accomplishment of yours."

Casually Lat Danziger tugged down his silk mask. Alex felt his spine start to crawl even before the disfigurement beneath was fully revealed. It was the mask, actually, that had betrayed Lat's identity. If he had not seen only Lat's eyes and recognized him thus, he would never have noticed his eyes for the gaunt horror below. Not a face—it could no longer be called a face.

It had been obvious on that long-ago day when the bullet-shattered lamp had exploded its clinging liquid fire full in the man's face that the resulting mutilation would be hideous . . . *but this.*

Again Lat laughed; but with full sight of the scarred gap that formed a noise of tinkling grace, the effect was indescribable. "An amusing sight for the post-breakfast hour, gentlemen, eh? My face received even less medication than my leg. A guard at the prison who couldn't bear the sight of me made the sight even more unbearable with periodic clubbings. Once I was on the outside, the result made living somewhat less than hell, but not by much. The ladies, you know, bless their hearts. It was long years, as you may imagine, before I learned to appreciate the ribald opportunities inherent in the situation. Since I had to wear a mask with even the ladies of Cypriot persuasions, the fees necessary to overcome their reluctance were considerable. One night the mask happened to slip." He grimaced with terrible laughter. "Under the circumstances, well, the lady's reaction was understandably extreme. Ah, but gratifying. Gentlemen, I can't forebear these antic qualms whenever I think of it."

"*Dios,*" Chino muttered. "I'm think you do yourself big favor if you laugh yourself to death."

"You're a kindred soul, Mr. Lucero. We are both clowns in life, but my funny face has yours beaten by all odds. But let me satisfy your curiosity, gentlemen—"

Alex, wondering how long they might stall him, put in, "What I don't understand is how you escaped prison without our hearing about it."

Lat grinned frightfully. "No escape, Mr. McKenna. I died there. I was assigned to the farm outside the walls, and attempted a break in company with three others. We were overtaken while crossing a river. Two of my companions were recaptured, one killed by gunfire. I feigned a fatal hit by going under, then letting the current carry me downstream. My body, of course, was never recovered, but to all intent I was killed attempting an escape. That was some six years ago."

"You waited a long time to set this up."

"Not really. Every man needs something to live for. The state of my face precluded any normal goals. That freed me to focus every attention on the matter of destroying Jonathan Trask. While engaging my fancy with delightful possibilities, I was in no hurry—and I needed a secure background for the work I had set myself to.

"I became Tigo. The vocation of a hired assassin in cattle wars fitted my talents and my plans, and let me avoid distressing prospects in rubbing elbows with humanity. I kept always to myself, living in the backcountry, developing plainscraft. Meantime I honed my tools on occasional jobs. There was a backwoods store where I purchased supplies; anybody wishing to contact me for professional purposes got a message to me through the storekeeper. A meeting was arranged, to which I always came masked as you've seen me. A suggestion of terror and mystery that helped promote many such a deal. My fees were such that I could have afforded to live resplendently in any world capital, but for—"

Tigo did not have to scowl to make his meaning clear; he only needed to smile. He smiled now, and went on, "When I felt the time was ripe, Mr. Trask, I came here. I learned of your squabble with some settlers and decided to turn your mild feud into a large one. They didn't send for me, you see; I sought them out and offered my services. I promised them only that I would stop you, not necessarily take your life. This dovetailed with my own plans—always collect a fee when and where you can, is my motto.

"To fill you with the taste of personal fear by an occasional ambush was a mere diversion. Every man has his calling. To a man of your gifts, nothing I could devise would stagger you as would the gradual, calculated destruction of all you had built. I started things moving toward that end.

"Then it occurred to me that isolating you from your empire, watching but unable to influence its course, was the way. Prison, of course. You would be helpless as a baby. No—paralyzed man would be better. A paralyzed man in possession of his faculties but unable to stir a muscle. A foretaste of hell to a man of your dispostion and energies.

"It was me, as you've by now guessed, who planted those hides on the Cady place, leaving a clear trail there. Then it was only a matter of staying in hiding close by to see what would develop. When your two brothers rode in to find the hides and accuse the Cadys, the hotheaded Cortney drew and fired on them. The Cadys returned fire, but apparently not to kill. I rectified that omission by shooting young Liam. My shot went unnoticed in the general rata-plan—evidently Cady believed either he or his son had found the mark, albeit by accident."

Jonathan said, *"You,"* and he was swaying on his feet. Alex had never seen anything hit him as Tigo's quiet words did. The blood had run out of his face; he looked gray and stunned, like a fighter on his last legs.

For the first time he was thrown face to face with the fact that he had committed his own raw brand of justice not on a pair of cattle thieves, not on his brother's murderers, but on two guiltless men, men innocent of either thievery or murder. Jonathan had never experienced a small emotion in his life; smallness was not in him, and Alex, seeing a doubt of depth seizing him for probably the first time in his life, thought, *My God—what must he be feeling?*

"You," Jonathan said in a strangling rasp, and cleared his throat. His voice was reedlike as he went on: "You must of done that other thing before—put them two rednecks in them green hides."

"Ah, the truth has bemused you—now you dig for further truth, is that it? Regrettably I did not commit that ingenious atrocity, which predated my arrival. A brillant and enviable stroke of—"

Jonathan wheeled suddenly, ignoring Tigo's uptilting rifle, hissing at Chino: "Straight now, Mex. Was it Cort? You was with him that day. Was it Cort killed them two in the hides?"

"Haaah. Why for all the sudden you got the taste to hear what really happen? You never want to hear it before."

"Answer me, God damn you!"

"All right, sure. I'm not there when it happen. Like it is told you, we split up to work, me, Cort an' Li. But later I'm come on what's happen. I find the two dead gringos in the hide. I find track all over that is plain. Cort done it. I mess up all the track so nobody know."

"God," Jonathan said.

"I'm ain't cover up to protect Cort. If I say truth,

Cort will deny her, hah? Then in gringo court it is word of Chino agains a white *Yanqui*. Haaah. I'm think I keep my mouth shut and keep my scalp. Anyway I'm think this is way the big Trask would want it." Chino gave a slight, expressive shrug. "Cort is drinking that day; he bring bottle along and he is pret' high. Maybe it is my fault for not taking bottle away, not keeping him in my sight, eh? I'm think of these things. Besides it ain' so bad killing a couple rustlers that way. She is the Spanish way. But you Anglos look at her wrong. No. Chino is thinking is wise to keep the mouth shut. Now you are ready hear truth, now I'm tell you truth."

"Truth, Mr. Lucero," Lat Danziger said, "is each man's perspective. Knowing what I did of Mr. Trask's, I had no need to hazard guesses as to his reaction. It was a predictable one. Having arranged that he blame the Cadys for his brother's death, I had only to let the law take its course."

Danziger's glance shifted grotesquely to Jonathan. "I was then content with images of you in prison—all perspective, you see? I couldn't guess that you were buoyed up, as surely you were, by a certainty that your release would be effected in a relatively short time. You can guess the rest—my chagrin on reading about your retrial, the resumption of my ravages of your material holdings. The '73 panic had already advanced the attrition of your former fortunes; I had only to abet the process. Then it was no trick of any magnitude to keep myself informed of the progress of your new trial and, when you were acquitted, to arrange today's diversion. You have been watched, gentlemen, since your departure from Saba City."

Alex said, "And now?"

"For you, Mr. McKenna—nothing. You once interceded to save my life. You did me no favor as you see, but your intention was honorable. You are free to ride away from here. I suggest that you do so at once."

"What are your plans for them?"

"You're trying my patience, Mr. McKenna." Danziger's voice crackled suddenly. "If you can look on this face and still ask that, you're a fool. I won't weary you with my plans for Mr. Trask, which involve a considerable detail. Mr. Lucero I owe neither grudge nor favor—I simply cannot afford to let him go. Several times in his dogging of my tracks, he came closer to me than he knew. He is a man of no little skill in shooting and tracking, therefore a danger to me." A pause, and Danziger said gently, "You, McKenna, cannot afford to be a fool. A twice-blessed man should think of his wife—his child."

Alex was thinking of them, and of something else. The pocket pistol he had discovered in his saddlebag at his first camp after leaving Katytown. JoAnne had urged him before his departure to take a pistol, but he hadn't carried one in years, and his rifle should be protection enough. A pistol was an invitation to trouble, he had told her; but she had stowed one in his gear anyway. On afterthought he'd been appreciative; he was inviting no difficulty with a concealed weapon, and it might come in handy.

Without a word now, he went to his horse, stepped into the saddle and rode slowly from the clearing, not looking back. There was perfect silence behind him, and he knew that Danziger would be listening to make sure he kept going.

When a thicket cut him off from view, Alex started undoing the flap of one saddlebag, holding his horse to a measured walk. And a last-minute qualm seized him. Why, with everything to live for, with a wife and a son dependent on him, should he risk his life to save two men who had no claim on his obligations? He remembered wryly his words to JoAnne, "I'll never take up with him or for him again," and thought, *"I've got to. It's the way I believe—she knows that better than anyone. Forgive me, Jo.*

He dived his hand into the saddlebag as he wheeled the horse on a tight rein; his hand dipped up the small caliber gun and he drummed his sorrel into a run back toward the clearing. Danziger would hear him coming, but there was no time for a stealthy approach. At least Danziger would not expect him to be armed; but then the little double-barreled British pistol would be useless as a popgun except at pointblank range, and probably he would not get that close.

But Chino, who fed on trouble, could be depended on to go into action like a blacksnake at the first opportunity. If he could give Chino that chance, they would all have a chance.

He raced through the mottled sunlight into the open. Lat Danziger was waiting for him, calmly swinging up his rifle. The little gun in Alex' fist spoke twice, like two flat whipcracks, and threw off Danziger's aim as he shot.

Alex felt the bullet smack into his horse's forequarters, and the animal was going forward and down. With the desperation of instinct rather than thought, Alex was flinging himself sideways even as the horse's stride broke. The world pinwheeled blindly; he struck full on his back with an impact that sent a wash of blackness across his mind.

The sensation lasted a broken instant—no longer, for his eyes flicked open in time to catch Chino in mid-lunge, and the big Mexican must have reacted almost at once. He had taken a step or two, then his spring-steel muscles launched him in a hurtling dive toward the guns Tigo had made them discard.

Snake-quick, Danziger had pivoted pulling his rifle around, and in the same second Alex' eyes came open, he shot hastily. A clean miss, and Chino hit the ground on his chest and belly with a savage grunt, an extended hand slapping over the butt of a pistol. He twisted catlike, coming half-up on his knees and elbows to whip the gun into line. Danziger barely got his rifle levered in the interim. The two shots lashed across each other, not merging but no breaking distinctly apart.

Danziger was jarred backward by the .45's impact, slamming against the big oak. His legs were buckling as he tried to bring the rifle up again, his face twisted in frightful agony. He began sliding down along the treetrunk. Sitting, he tried sluggishly again to raise his rifle, and this time nearly succeeded. Then his head canted over and his eyes shaded into glassy fixity—he died that way, cramped against the tree with his knees drawn up.

Chino's face had dropped into the earth after he fired the one shot. Danziger's second bullet had hammered down into his back, killing him instantly.

22

IT SEEMED A LONG TIME BEFORE JONATHAN moved, going over to Chino, bending down beside him. He laid a hand on the dead man's back. "Chino," he said. "Mex." There was no particular tone in his voice.

Alex climbed slowly to his feet, moving his legs and arms gingerly, finding with a mild astonishment that he had broken no bones in his fall. He felt numb and shaken, but that was reaction to the flurry of violence that had left two dead men in its wake. *Two more dead men,* he thought, looking at Jonathan. *Funny he can walk any more, the string of dead men he's wearing around his neck.*

At last, working his legs as slowly and stiffly as a man waking from a long sleep, Jonathan got to his feet. He looked at Alex with eyes that were strangely blank. "You didn't need to come back." He spoke with a distant, fumbling care, as if each word had demanded a conscious effort. "Seems you never could resist taking a hand when you been needed, boy."

Then his thoughts wrenched back to the real object of his concentration. His eyes were still fixed on Alex, but did not see him at all. "Cort," he murmured. "It was Cort really to blame all along, wa'nt it? It was Cort killed them two rednecks with the hides. That was where it started."

Alex watched him, feeling a faint alarm. "No. It started a long time before that."

Jonathan seemed not to hear him. "It was Cort pushed them Cadys into a gunfight, then lied about it."

"You believed him," Alex said quietly. "It was you that went bellering and pawing off after the Cadys. They were strung up on your orders. Give Lat Danziger a vote of credit, too."

"Cort lied," Jonathan went on in the soft, insistent voice of a man working himself toward a focus of intense certainty. "Cort lied to me from the beginning, or nothing Danziger could of done would of worked out. All his life I sheltered him like a baby. I paid off for his skylarkings. I shielded his hide from anyone and everyone who had reason for nailing it up. There ain't nothing left. The GT is ruint, the Mex is dead. There ain't nothing, and all because of that God damn boy."

"Danziger said something about perspective. Did you hear him?"

Jonathan said thickly, "What?"

"The cynic's definition of truth. He said truth was each man's perspective. Your perspective was that Cort could do no wrong. Now, all of a sudden, Cort is to blame for everything."

Talking to Jonathan, he saw, was like grabbing at a greased pig; his words were sliding off Jonathan's frame of mind to no purpose. With a touch of desperation he went on quickly, "But suppose there's a lot more to truth? More than a man can ever know totally, but enough to let him take a long stride past the childish error of settling on any single person or event as a point of origin—fixing all blame there?"

Jonathan scowled suddenly. "You know I never liked that muddy God damn kind of talk."

Alex nodded calmly. "You always were afraid of it as I recall."

"I never been afraid of a God damn thing!"

"No, not of anything you could lay both hands on and tie knots in, whether it was moneymaking or stringing up somebody you decided was in your way. But you were always afraid of a thought, Buck. A thought can topple a thousand bigotries and righteous self-justifications. It can change a man's whole life in less time than it takes to wink an eye. One thought can make it clear as glass that Cort, poor sorry Cort, is just a weak, wild kid."

"That's what I been saying!" Jonathan roared.

"Yes, years after I told you the same thing. A simple, declared fact that you wouldn't see because you didn't want to. Just as now you don't want to see the rest of it—the way Cort just emulated the biggest thing in his young life. You. If this creed became ruthless self-interest, where did he get it from? You. Oh, you never lied or sneaked; you always shot your dogs for the whole world to see. That was your rule of personal strength and pride. But what have rules to do with a weakling like Cort? Man, Cort could never be anything of himself—he could only follow. He could only imitate his big brother's passions, never his codes. Why do you think you always had to stand between Cort and the consequences of his acts? Where does blame begin when—"

"*Shut up!*" Jonathan seemed to tower in his wrath, his great fists flexing open and shut. His eyes were maniacal; an over-powering intensity was bursting in him.

Abruptly he swung on his heel and ran to his horse, throwing himself into the saddle almost before his foot was secure in the stirrup. Turning the animal, he kicked it furiously into an all-out run, cutting west on the sedgegrass plain, straight as a die toward Katytown.

For a moment Alex stood motionless in his dismay.

Had he gone too far in in his urge to shake Jonathan into a realization, finally, of the whole truth? The answer came to him almost as one with the question. No, he had tried to divert something that was building to a swift, feral head and had failed, that was all.

Jonathan's strength was all of a kind. He could master anything that demanded only a blunt, single decision backed by insensitive force or a show of it. The trouble was, he saw all of life in the same simplistic terms, a wrong set of terms. The complexities involved in realistic living were infinite, and to a perceptive man who could escape the corrosion of cynicism, this same complexity gave life a richness and variance that made it worth the candle. Jonathan had all of an instinctual man's appreciation of the sensual fullness of existence, but he lacked the perceptive man's eye to uncompromising reality.

A single crack in the dyke of his stubborn self-conviction was more than his nature could accommodate. What he had really seen was not Cort's general worthlessness and perfidy—for a part of his mind could not have failed to acknowledge these things all along—but rather the monumental process of his own self-deception over the years. This being more than he could fully admit, he had turned his fury against Cort.

What did he intend doing now? Alex did not know, nor what might be done to stop it, but he expected the worst. With a driving urgency in him, he looked at his own dead horse, then at Chino's mount. Nobody but its late master had ever stayed on that rawboned brute, but he spent several futile minutes in making the attempt. Then, remembering the whicker made by Lat Danziger's concealed horse, he made a hasty search of the nearby thickets.

The animal, a splendid and tractable bay, stood quietly as he mounted, responding beautifully to his touch. In a moment Alex was riding away from the motte and the two sprawled, silent bodies.

He set a swift pace for town, but Jonathan kept well ahead of him. Alex could see the horse and rider, a black static dot on the tawny plain. And the dot vanished at last behind a long swell on the undulating prairie. Only two miles beyond that height of land was Katytown, and Jonathan got there minutes ahead of him.

Alex was on the outskirts of town before he remembered that Jonathan had taken off in his blind haste without retrieving the pistol Danziger had made him discard. Alex thought of Jonathan's present temper, of his probably intention of confronting Cort, and of the quick-triggered wildness that was Cort's typical response to a prodding.

Thinking of these things, Alex didn't slacken his pace as he rode into town. He held the bay to a hard clip as he swerved through three residential blocks to reach the old main street. If Jonathan were looking for his brother, remembering what Alex had said about Cort's recent debauchery, he would head by instinct for the Steerhead Bar, the Trasks' favorite watering place for years.

Jonathan's horse, he saw, was tied at the rack in front; but even as Alex veered that way, the shot came, high and hollow, beating down the midday quiet.

Men were already coverging on the Steerhead as Alex reached the porch, but he was first through the saloon doors.

Jonathan lay face down on the floor, and Cort was sagging against the bar, his back to it. The gun he had used was slipping from his fingers, and it clattered on the floor as Alex stepped inside and halted. Cort's face was pasty with bewilderment and fright. The wildness and marks of low living were momentarily erased for